Maxi's Place:

Rumors Ring True
It's Complicated
The Lies We Tell

Literary Stud

Rumors Ring True

*Reading is a majority skill
but a minority art.
— Julian Barnes*

DEDICATION

This book is dedicated to my family: my parents for nurturing a writer's soul, my brother for supporting me through anything I've attempted to do and my sister, the epitome of a best friend.

To my fiancée, for putting up with my manic moments with patience, understanding and unconditional love.

*To Wilmer.
I hope you enjoy
the read.*

Rumors Ring True

CONTENTS

Rumors Ring True

ACKNOWLEDGMENTS

A special thanks to my team of editors for their diligence and hard work.

Trasie Banks

Regina Thomas

Michele Appello

Cover Photo:
Dallas Skyline
Robert Hensley

Episode One: Rumors Ring True

CHAPTER 1

Summer in Dallas, Texas was not a season to be taken lightly. The heat was confusing as one moment it was dry and the next, steaming rain rolled through, ruining the hair plans of quite a few women. The heat didn't stop weekend revelers from stepping out into the humidity for some entertainment. Clubs and restaurants rose to the challenge of cooling off a cranky hoard. Maxi's Place, located on the outskirts of downtown, pushed frozen alcoholic drinks the moment customers began streaming in the double doors. The fruity concoctions hampered the crowd's impatience as they waited for their little buzzers to vibrate and flash red.

Ava smiled at a foursome of merry diners as she led them through the restaurant to their designated table. After presenting them with the menu, she glanced at the stage. The jazz quintet, *Thompson 5*, played every weekend and was one of the reasons why Maxi's Place was so popular. Featuring cool and Cuban jazz, they had a loyal following. Even Ava owned a couple of their underground CDs and was excited when she applied for a job at the host stand. She chanced a peek at the tall, lanky individual playing the saxophone. Her cheeks were puffed out, causing a soulful wail to filter out among the listeners. With closed eyes, Bailey Thompson let the music take control, beads of perspiration coating her forehead.

Bailey's solo ended and Ava quickly returned to the host stand to seat another table, colliding with Cole Washington, the owner and manager. Cole raised her eyebrows at Ava before moving through the throng of people. She admonished herself for thinking about Bailey - again. Since she began working at Maxi's a month ago, Ava resisted the urge to behave like a devoted fan. Warned by the entire host stand, the wait staff, and the musicians, Ava heeded their advice. College during the day and working night's left little time for sleep, much less dating. However, Ava couldn't help noticing the confidence that Bailey exuded when she was on stage. A mysterious, fascinating side of Bailey teased the crowd when she caressed her saxophone. Ava was intrigued but didn't reveal her attraction to anyone at the restaurant and kept her distance. She focused again on the busy night happening around her. At the end of her shift, Ava leaned against the bar waiting for the to-go food she'd ordered. She had stepped out of one shoe to flex her toes and didn't notice Bailey appear by her side.

"Mountain Dew to go please, Logan." Bailey requested, an unlit Black & Mild cigar clenched between her teeth.

Struck mute, Ava tried not to stare like an idiot. She admired Bailey's taper fade haircut and the way her lips were full and fleshy. Ava shifted her gaze to the empty tables and employees in various stages of cleaning.

"You're new, right?"

Ava's head slowly turned toward Bailey's raspy voice. "Are you speaking to me?"

Bailey's grin was crooked. "Uh yeah. Bailey Thompson."

Ava accepted her outstretched hand, noticing how soft it was. "Ava. It's nice to meet you."

"You too." Bailey shifted and sipped her soda before speaking again. "You need to get more comfortable shoes if you're going to stomp around this place."

"I know. I haven't had the time to shop for them." Ava slipped her shoe back on.

"Trust me. Your feet will thank you for it." Bailey nodded. "I waited tables here for three years. Every night for the first few weeks,

I would go home with aching feet until I found the right shoes. I still bought gel in-soles for extra insurance."

"Daniel told me about a shoe store with affordable, slip-resistant shoes. I was going there." Ava didn't know why they were having this conversation.

"I know the spot he's talking about. You should find something. Well, I'm off to my humble dwelling." Bailey saluted with her saxophone case leaving Ava a bit confused.

Ava didn't see Bailey again until the next weekend. She didn't want to admit that she'd looked for her during her shifts all week. Happy hour had not yet begun and there was a lull of working silence as employees prepared the evening's atmosphere. Bailey stepped on stage while Ava checked menu baskets. She stopped to watch her flex the tone holes of the tenor saxophone. The sharp creases of her starched jeans and long-sleeved green shirt were a complete opposite of the ballad she began to play. Bailey left her shirt unbuttoned, revealing a white A-shirt and a simple, silver labrys lying against her smooth chocolate skin. Mesmerized, Ava imagined those lean fingers pushing and pulling her into submission. Suddenly, Bailey looked up and met Ava's gaze, greeting her with a wink. Knowing she shouldn't have, Ava smiled a response before continuing on. Throughout the night, she continued to connect with Bailey and didn't stop her bold eye flirting.

"Need an escort to your car, ma'am?" Bailey appeared at Ava's side while she rummaged through her purse looking for her keys.

"Um, sure." Ava's heart rate increased. "As soon as I find my keys."

"Maybe if you carried something smaller than a suitcase you could find them." She teased.

"Oh, don't you talk about my purse now." Ava's fingers finally wrapped around the defiant objects. "Everyone can't carry all they need in their back pocket."

"I'll concede that." Bailey saw the ever-watchful Daniel standing at the host stand.

"Thank you." Ava caught Daniel's smirk before she hurried out the door.

Bright lights of a passing vehicle washed over them as they walked to the parking garage in silence. Bailey felt unusually nervous after flirting with Ava most of the night. The same tingles that overtook her body before stepping on stage coursed through her veins now. When they reached Ava's small, conservative sedan, Bailey acknowledged the awkward moments.

"Excuse me for talking your ear off." She said.

"Yeah, I was going to say something about that." Ava tossed her purse into the car. "So did you have a purpose for walking me to my car?"

Bailey leaned into Ava. "You know I did."

"What was your purpose?" She could smell the masculine fragrance Bailey wore.

"I wanted to talk to you."

"For what?" Ava tried nonchalance.

"We locked eyes all night. Something is happening between us. Let's grab a cup of coffee and get to know each other better." Bailey licked her lips.

Ava fought against the urge to agree. "Do you really think that's a good idea?"

Bailey shrugged her shoulders. "Why wouldn't it be?"

"We work together. It could cause conflict." She rationalized.

"That sounds more like an excuse than a reason." Bailey said. "What's the story, Ava?"

Briefly distracted by hearing her name, Ava said the first thing that popped in her head. "I've been warned about you."

Bailey cursed the day Daniel applied for a job. The gossip floated around the restaurant ever since. "Shouldn't you get to know me first before you listen to idle chatter?"

"So what I've heard isn't true?" She held her breathe and prayed.

"I don't know. What have you heard?"

Ava sighed. "Thank you for the invitation but since we work together I don't think it would be a good idea."

"You're right. Have a good night." Bailey walked away without a backwards glance.

CHAPTER 2

Fish problems were not Daniel's forte. He didn't believe in concerning himself with Lesbians and their many emotions. However, out of sheer boredom on a slow night, he picked up on the open hostility between Bailey and Ava. The first clue was when Bailey made a point of visiting the host stand to ask a question. Laying out the charm to another hostess, Bailey couldn't help glancing at Ava. The next night, Daniel caught Bailey staring from the bar, eyes smoldering as they followed Ava around the restaurant. Two nights later, Ava collided with Bailey at the front door. She caught Ava to keep her from tumbling to the floor. Bailey held her for a moment before letting go. Ava's eyes were wide, lips parted as though she was about to speak. Bailey chose not to acknowledge it, bowed to her instead while holding open the door. Turning around, she caught Daniel being nosey.

"Don't you have something to do?" Bailey growled, stalking past.

"Looks like you're not getting anywhere with that one, Bailey Bear. Rejection must be difficult for you." Daniel taunted.

Bailey stopped and walked back to the host stand. "You don't know anything about me, Daniel. Not a muthafuckin' thing. And stop fucking calling me Bailey Bear."

"You know I may not know a lot about you but what I do know is what is keeping that fish to herself." Daniel loved to get into the mix of everything. Gossip was his favorite pastime. Well, that and sexy men.

"What did you tell her?" Bailey was surprised she cared. Ava was just another piece of ass.

"I told her the truth, Bailey Bear. I told her how new hostesses always quit their jobs after dating you for a few weeks. I told her how they cried themselves stupid waiting on your call." Daniel grinned.

"Were you there, Daniel? I don't recall you in my fuckin' house while I was dating these women. You need to mind your own fucking business." Bailey turned on her heels and stomped to the stage. She nodded at Cole as she unpacked her saxophone. So it was Daniel, with his bitch ass. The last thing she needed was for his diarrhea of the mouth to get around to the wrong people. Unfortunately, it looked like it already had. One of those damned hostesses adorned her with the idiotic nickname. She couldn't even remember which one. Bailey licked her lips, caressed her instrument, and blew a woeful ballad through its brass body. Cole sat down at the table in front to listen.

She nodded when Bailey finished. "That was smooth."

"Thank you." She sat down at the table, resting her sax on top. "Something I've been working on."

"I see you've been working on something else too." Cole slipped the comment across the table and dared Bailey to pick it up.

"What do you mean, Cole?" Bailey held her breathe. Diarrhea of the mouth.

"I'm through losing hostesses, Bailey. I finally have just enough and I don't need you messing with that, you hear me?" Cole hated laying down the law. Bailey just exhibited her charm and impetuous flair too much.

"No, I hear you. Trust me, Cole. I'm not fucking with nobody up here." The sad part was that she was telling the truth, something that didn't happen often.

"Alright, I'm trusting you on that, son. Don't let me down." Cole leaned over and playfully slapped her face.

"I got you, Cole." Bailey watched Cole stride to a trim and proper woman standing by the bar. Cole led her toward the office at the back of the restaurant. Boss Lady never minded mixing business and pleasure. Bailey scowled at Daniel who was smirking and examining his nails. Trick ass muthafucka.

CHAPTER 3

The booming music of the strip club pounded in Bailey's ears. She swirled the ice in her empty glass and debated whether she wanted another drink. She was tired of the scantily clad women and made a quick exit, disappointed that the end result was lackluster. The distraction, once so dependable, didn't keep Ava from scampering through her mind. Her charm failed to make Ava throw caution to the wind and that fact was haunting. Bailey couldn't understand why she cared about some chick who didn't want to date her. The fact that Ava would listen to the idle chatter floating around the restaurant was infuriating. She thought Ava had too much class to fall into that trap. It didn't matter if some of it was the truth. Bailey thought ogling some beautiful, big-breasted, thick-hipped creatures of dancing delight would take her mind off of the frustration. However, for the first time in ages, the ladies did nothing for her but seem more than a little distant. Now if Ava danced for her...Bailey shrugged off the vision.

The certainty of boredom at home had Bailey wandering the streets in the wee hours of the morning in search of any sort of distraction. Nights were always long and lonely when you were preoccupied with your love life. Bailey passed by a 24-hour porn shop and made a u-turn. It had been a while since she marveled at the different types of satisfaction paraphernalia available to consumers. The bright fluorescent lights temporarily blinded her as she stepped through the door. She nodded at the security guard leaning on the counter as she passed. Techno music blared through the speakers surrounding the fetish establishment. Bailey wandered through the aisles of DVDs, glancing at a few of the Lesbian titles. Some of the photos on the boxes had her shaking her head, happy she decided long ago to shop at an online specialty store. Bailey moved to the toy section stopping to check the price of a leather strap harness that caught her eye. She was inspecting the quick release on the sides when someone tapped her shoulder.

"Fancy meeting you here." Ava tried to appear nonchalant, but when she saw Bailey browsing the porn collection, her heart smashed against her rib cage.

"This is a coincidence."

"Do you always frequent porn shops this early in the morning?"

"Not every day, no." Bailey laughed.

Ava smiled, feeling mischievous after noticing the harness Bailey was holding. "So did your other strap break?"

"Uh, no. I was just taking a look at it for a future buy." She smiled crookedly and replaced the leather object on the display pegs.

"I guess one should always plan ahead." Ava commented. "Are you researching, um, attachments as well?"

"I have heard that's a good idea." Bailey followed her to the colorful wall of dildos and magic eggs.

Ava picked up an extra-large, lime green dick. The advertising guaranteed a realistic feel. "I don't understand why they have to be so big."

"Because the manufacturers think that your pussy can fit a locomotive." Bailey replied. "If you're shopping, go for what you think would fit comfortably."

Ava blushed. "Oh I wasn't in the market for one. I've never even used one before."

"Really? What are you shopping for?" She asked.

The blush deepened. "Um, well…my personal massager broke."

Bailey stifled a giggle. "Wow. Were you in the middle of…?"

"Smack dab in the middle." Ava replied. They both erupted in laughter drawing curious stares from other patrons.

"Have you found one you like yet? Or will you get the same one again?" Bailey asked, still snickering.

"I did get the same one. Why change what works?" Ava showed her the shopping basket holding the small, pink vibrator with bunny ears.

"True that."

"So how do you know so much about choosing a dildo?" She tugged on Bailey's coat sleeve.

"I've helped pick out a couple." Bailey admitted.

"Oh." Ava replaced the neon dildo on the wall. "I've never used one before."

"You said that. That's a shame." Bailey fixed her bedroom eyes on her. "I think you would enjoy it."

Ava felt bold. "I'm sure with the right person I would enjoy it."

"Maybe I can help you out with that." Bailey moved closer to Ava, inhaling the flowery aroma of her body wash.

Ava's breath caught in her throat. The unfulfilled ardor that had sent her out into the night burned anew. How ironic that it was Bailey she was thinking about when that damn vibrator conked out on her. "Maybe you could."

Bailey's jaw dropped. That wasn't the answer she was expecting. "Did you just throw me a curveball?"

"I might have." She answered. This has to be fate. Ava couldn't stop thinking about Bailey and was near submission earlier at the restaurant. They had bumped full body into each other and when she lost footing and almost fell, Bailey caught her. Ava almost melted when those eyes held a glimpse of concern. That gaze was icy a split-second later when Bailey let go. Ava didn't think her feelings could be so hurt.

"So what's the story, Ava?"

She swallowed at the crow stuck in her throat and suddenly everything spilled forth in a rush of words. "I lied to you when I said I wasn't interested. It was wrong of me to assume anything about you especially when I didn't know you. I never should have listened to Daniel. He just likes to stir up drama. I can't stop thinking about you. I've tried. It's just...well, do you think we could do this low-key? I mean, not let it get around the restaurant?"

"Oh, so now that you can't stop thinking about a nigga, you want to hook up?" Bailey's question stung. "You don't think I may have changed my mind at this point?"

"I deserve that. You're right. I should have given you a chance." Ava nodded, looking away so Bailey wouldn't see her eyes water. She was thinking of an escape route when Bailey leaned toward her lightly kissing her. Ava clutched at Bailey, holding her close to deepen the kiss. Bailey slipped her tongue between Ava's lips and the surroundings drifted away as denied passion consumed them both.

"Hey you two! I love the show but you're going to have to take it somewhere else." The attendant behind the counter called out. Bailey and Ava broke apart, breathing heavily.

Ava was the first to speak. "I didn't mean to lose control like that."

"But you did." Bailey reached for her hand.

"Yes, I did." Ava loved the softness of her skin.

"So which one would you get?" Bailey gestured to the wall.

"Um." She studied the pleasure giving objects. One that was medium sized and a caramel color stood out the most. Ava thought it would match Bailey's skin tone perfectly. "I like this one."

Bailey reached for the package. "Alright. This one it is."

"What are you doing?" Ava hadn't expected Bailey to call her bluff.

"I'm buying this." Bailey answered. "I think at this stage in our acquaintance we should exchange numbers."

"You think so?" Ava was already reaching into her purse. "Why is that?"

"I'd like to get to know you a little better before we take this for a spin." Bailey replied.

Ava was impressed and aroused. "W-What a good idea."

"Okay. Why don't we pay for these items and go get a quick bite to eat." Bailey licked her lips and smiled.

CHAPTER 4

The black, plastic bag hung between them and every few seconds a breeze would pass through making the plastic crinkle. Ava agreed to follow Bailey across the street to the all night restaurant specializing in breakfast food. Giddy with excitement, she hummed and chair danced until parking again. Bailey entwined her fingers with Ava's as they walked into the restaurant lobby. From all the flirting and innuendoes, the waitress felt she was intruding while taking their order.

"I don't know much about you, Ava." Bailey said suddenly, pushing her plate aside.

"I don't know much about you either, Bailey." She countered.

"I asked first."

"What do you want to know?"

"You want something specific?" Bailey stalled. "What's your favorite color?"

"Very deep question. Emerald green." Ava smiled. "Anything else?"

"Well, you put me on the spot."

"Well, when you say something like you don't know much about a person, I assumed you wanted to know something specific." Ava explained.

Bailey nodded. "True. Being completely honest, most women offer at least a paragraph about their likes and dislikes."

"I will agree that most women would. However, I don't normally prepare a speech about my likes and dislikes." She informed Bailey. "But just for you, I will give it a try."

"I appreciate it."

"No problem. Now, let's see. Dislikes are easier. I don't like bullies or pushy people. I love ambition though. I just think there is a difference. Drinking out of the container is a big pet peeve as well leaving the cabinets open in the kitchen." Ava shrugged at Bailey's smirk. "I don't know why, it just is."

"Any sexual dislikes I should know about?" Bailey asked.

"Don't worry. You'll find out." Ava replied. "We're getting to know each other first, right?"

"Of course we are. If you recall, it was my idea." She shifted her right leg so that it rubbed against Ava's.

"I do recall that." Ava fought an excited tremor.

"How about a movie on Saturday when we get off work?"

"At two in the morning?" Ava shook her head. "How about Tuesday? I think we're both off."

Bailey consented. "Tuesday it is."

Walking back to their cars, they chatted about the night's events.

"You do understand why I want to keep this between us, right?" Ava asked.

"Of course I do. You're ashamed to be seen with me."

"That's not true."

Bailey laughed. "I know. I know. It's because Daniel has diarrhea of the mouth."

Ava smiled. "That's disgusting."

"But true."

"Well, Boss Lady warned you too."

Bailey shook her head. "Yeah, she wouldn't be too happy with me. I don't like my business out in the street anyway."

"Exactly." Ava grabbed Bailey's jacket, pulling her close for a kiss. She pushed her away before she changed her mind.

"Well damn."

"I'm glad I ran into you tonight."

"Me too. Be expecting my call."

Ava smirked at the cocky instruction. "Just make sure you call."

Bailey wasted no time calling her. After making sure Ava arrived home safely, she chatted for another twenty minutes before hanging up. No point in seeming too eager. Sexual energy ravaged her body as she lay awake, humming a golden melody while her mind raced. Ava's request about their dating status was a surprise. Usually she was the one with that stipulation. Bailey didn't think Ava was the playa type and decided not to think too much into it, instead shifting to how beautiful her brown eyes were. Bailey hadn't ever felt mesmerized before, but Ava had a way of holding her gaze like no one had before. She was truly a pleasure to talk to and Bailey found it refreshing that she had a healthy appetite. Bailey grinned. That girl could put away some French toast. Finally dozing off, she recalled the silky feel of those full lips.

The next morning, Bailey called Ava to wish her a good day. She turned on the charm, finalizing their date plans and dropped subtle innuendoes. After an hour, they finally got around to discussing their down-low agreement.

"I think we should just go on as before." Ava suggested. "We'll ignore each other and no one will catch on."

"That sounds like a plan." Bailey agreed. "It also means you'll have to control your urges."

She giggled. "My urges? What urges are you talking about?"

"You can't look at me with those beautiful, brown eyes, beckoning me with an invitation."

"Is that what I do?"

"Yeah, that's what you do. So you better control yourself."

"I don't think I'm the one that needs reminding."

"You don't?"

"No, I don't. You're obviously obsessed with my beautiful, brown eyes and hoping there is an invitation." Ava said.

Bailey chuckled. "That may be so but I'll get an invitation one day."

CHAPTER 5

Bailey invaded Ava's thoughts for the rest of the day. She questioned the whimsical sentiments swirling around and they hadn't gone on a date yet. Becoming a notch on Bailey's strap didn't fit in her life goals but Ava had a weakness for the bad boi type. She always made a pact with her heart not to get hurt again but the inevitable always seemed to sneak up on her. Having difficulty concentrating on studying at the university library, she escaped for a cup of coffee. Ava daydreamed about the moment she saw Bailey at the porn shop. Ava watched her stroll around the DVD library for about ten minutes. With fluid mannerisms and an unmistakable swagger, Bailey kept the audience enthralled whenever she stepped on stage. Ava mustered up the courage for an approach before she was noticed. Her emotions fought with her judgment. Nevertheless, Ava took their meeting as fate and welcomed the chance to lay some questions to rest.

Later, Cole made her usual double check of the reservation book, when Bailey strolled in. Ava wanted to run up and hug her but looked away. She felt Cole's eyes for most of the night whenever

Bailey crossed her path and knew they made the right decision about anonymity. There were just too many Bailey haters lurking around, searching for the opportunity to stir up trouble. Ava couldn't afford trouble. She had bills and tuition to pay. This was a good job for being part-time and she loved the atmosphere. Ava finally felt comfortable with her choices in life. She hoped she made the right decision. It was definitely one she hadn't thought about long enough. Bailey's reputation preceded her at every turn. Ava was aware of the *Thompson 5* groupies who made sure to be in attendance at every performance. Bailey was a favorite among the Lesbian fans and always gave her public the attention they yearned for. Ava witnessed numbers slipped in Bailey's hand or an invitation of some after-hour pleasure. She wondered how many of these women received an occasional late night call. Ava vowed she wouldn't be caught slipping and set a time limit on having sex. Bailey could roll along if she wanted.

The night of their date, Ava changed clothes four times. She settled on a summer dress with a short jacket. Surprisingly punctual, Bailey brought Ava flowers and remarked how beautiful she was out of uniform. She opened the passenger side of the two-door coupe and waited until Ava adjusted before closing the door. Bailey explained that she didn't want to accidently bump into anyone and drove to a restaurant in a different part of town, set in an outdoor mall. They walked hand in hand through the pavilion past a huge, stone fountain. Water cascaded down and every once in a while a breeze would splash the children running around. Impressed with Bailey's choice, Ava admired the relaxed ambiance and beautiful decorations. She hadn't expected Bailey to be witty and easy to talk to.

"So what's your major?" Bailey pushed aside the menu and focused all her attention on Ava.

"You've asked about me, huh?" Ava teased.

"I might have." She grinned. "You weren't exactly talking to me."

"We weren't talking to each other." Ava corrected. "Anyway, my major is marketing and accounting."

"That's a lot of homework."

"My time is rather limited."

"In that case, I'm honored to be fit into your busy schedule."

She blushed. "My pleasure."

Bailey smiled. "You also like to read."

"Are you stalking me?"

"Do you usually have stalkers?"

"Not usually."

"Then I don't think you have anything to be afraid of."

It was Ava's turn to smile. "Well, what do I like to read?"

Bailey chuckled. "I didn't get that part. I kind of overheard the conversation."

"The truth comes out." She teased. "You didn't ask about me. You eavesdropped."

"You got me." She lifted her hands in surrender. "Most women would ask who was talking about them."

Ava shook her head. "Sweetie, you'll find out I'm not like most women."

"I'm looking forward to it."

After dinner, they walked around the pavilion, talking some more and enjoying the night air. The evening took Ava by surprise and the tingly feeling she had all day grew stronger by the minute. Instead of succumbing to her hormones, she renewed her determination to stick to her rules and remembered that this was a first date. On the way home, a smooth R&B melody filtered out of the car speakers. Ava smirked, thinking that Bailey was laying it on thick. Every track involved a sexual theme, and soon erotic images of Bailey danced around her head. She imagined toned arms wrapped around her waist, holding her tight. Ava knew those silky lips would drive her crazy. A tell-tale sensation spread to her thighs and she quickly changed her line of thinking. *What if she tries to kiss me? What if she doesn't?* She responded to Bailey's comments about the poets as they strolled to her front door, hand in hand. Ava steeled herself, sure that this was the moment Bailey would make her move.

"Thanks for your time, Ava." Bailey grinned. "I know how important it is."

Ava smirked. "Yes, it is but I think I made the right choice in spending it with you."

"I think so too."

Bailey pulled her close. Ava's eyes fluttered but, instead felt a light kiss on her cheek and a quick hug. She wished Ava a good night's rest, waiting until the lock clicked before walking away. Bewildered,

Ava watched her lean form through the peephole. She smiled. *Maybe she's different after all*

CHAPTER 6

Restaurant employees were a breed all their own. Much akin to a dysfunctional family, highs and lows happened on a daily basis. Various cliques cropped up with every new hire orientation and civil wars were normal. A few employees were married, some had children but most were young and undisciplined. Cole's no dating policy was broken all the time and she only stepped in when drama erupted, which was often. To stay ahead of the game, she paid attention to the gossip and rumors floating around. Even though various ass kissers kept her informed, Cole trusted her intuition more. She didn't need anyone to point out Bailey and Ava's exaggerated performance. Their charade of ignoring each other's presence wasn't obvious to others but Cole felt a fire and intensity between them. Tasha thought she was crazy and told her so every time she brought it up.

"I think you're imagining things." She had a kitchen to get back to and no time for Cole's intuition. Tasha was sure the sous chefs were messing something up. "Can we get back to the menu?"

Cole shuffled the stack of recipes Tasha brought her. She couldn't shake that feeling. "I told Bailey to stay away from Ava."

Tasha sighed. "Well, no one can dictate love. Not even you."

"I'm not trying to dictate love. I don't want drama in my restaurant." She leaned back in the chair and put her polished Stacy Adams up on the desk. "It's bad for business."

"I agree, but…"

"I don't like buts."

"That's a lie." Tasha grinned. "Anyway, why don't you leave it alone until absolutely necessary?"

"I don't like being lied to, Tasha." Cole replied.

"No one is lying to you, Cole. They're being discreet." Tasha stood, plucked the recipes out of her hand and started toward the door.

"I didn't approve those yet."

"You took too long. Don't worry. I got this."

"It better be good." She warned, appreciating her round backside swishing away.

"Don't tell me how to run my kitchen." Tasha retorted. "And stop looking at my ass."

Cole remembered her comment later when she passed through the kitchen. "Your kitchen is in my restaurant."

Tasha rolled her eyes. "Don't start with me, Cole. The salad station is behind and pasta ran out of penne."

"Well, I'm sure you can handle it." She grinned. "After all, it is your kitchen."

"I hope you get heartburn."

Cole exited before Tasha thought of anymore curses and took a turn around the main dining area. The band was on a break and muffled jazz music piped in through the surround sound speakers. Soft lights were brought up to allow diners a little conversation and a refill on drinks. Cole stopped at a few tables, working the regulars in the room with a few handshakes and smiles. She scanned the scurrying employees for productivity while walking to the host stand. Checking the wait time, she noticed Bailey leaning against the bar, staring off into space. Cole followed the trail of eyes, stopping at Ava wiping down the glass front door. She obviously wasn't paying attention to the smudges as she met Bailey's intense gaze. Tasha would be in the kitchen when Cole had obvious proof.

There were two ways this could play out. The relationship might have a happily-ever-after ending, true love overcoming and all that. Or Cole would have a mess to clean up at some point. She contemplated her options and Tasha's discreet label kept intruding in the thought process. Cole knew Bailey's rumored reputation was fact and so far, Ava seemed to have a good head on her shoulders. Their coupling might bring static to the laid back ambiance although, so far they kept it tightly under wraps. She had to admit their plan was a bit clever but knew that the best laid plans often backfired. Cole sighed heavily and retreated to the office for a quick drink. After a few sips of cognac, her head cleared and she decided to follow Tasha's advice. She'd wait for them to fuck it up and then step in. Tasha was usually right. Cole would never tell her though.

CHAPTER 7

Bailey kept a mental checklist of how to woo Ava. She'd dated the nerdy type before and charted a course through familiar waters. Women always melted for the tortured artist. Bailey wasn't exactly tortured but she knew what game she was working with. Some had words. Others had swag. She had music and the ladies ate it up every chance she gave them. First, appealing to Ava's intellectual side, Bailey took care in choosing where their dates were, knowing she wasn't a movie and a dinner chick. She doled out as much attention as possible without becoming a stalker, memorizing all pertinent information such as likes and dislikes, what made her tear up and her motivations in life. Ava's wall slowly crumbled and their conversations entered a deep phase lasting for hours. When the texts began to include hugs, kisses and I miss you's, Bailey stepped up the romance with flowers and old fashioned gallantry.

The few times their dates became passionate, Bailey backed off first, watching Ava's eyes light up with untamed ardor. Her pride was still hurt from public rejection and influenced the decision that Ava was going to have to ask for it. Bailey would do everything she could to make it happen. She wondered what type of lover this conservative woman would be. Was Ava a moaner? A screamer? Bailey hoped she wasn't a pillow princess. Sex was more fun with participation. A month passed before she felt Ava was ripe for the taking and decided to give her a little push. Located in a hole in the wall bar, they passed judgment on the various artists and their poetry at a spoken word competition. The intricate phrases touched Ava while Bailey commented more on the musical accompaniment. She scooted closer, draping an arm across the back of Ava's chair. Bailey touched her throughout the show, whether it was holding her hand or caressing her cheek.

Ava inhaled her tantalizing cologne and fought the sensation between her legs. No one in her past came close to invoking a longing within her like Bailey did. Ava usually followed a set of standards and nearly cast them away every time she was with Bailey. Her new vibrator received a lot more action these days but she couldn't make the first move. Ava didn't know how to be aggressive with sex. Her few past lovers were aggressive enough and she'd grown accustomed to dropping little hints without actually saying what she wanted. However, Bailey wasn't picking up on any of her clues, leaving Ava a bit frustrated. She didn't dare ask about the strap but often fantasized about how Bailey would look in it. She wondered if she'd like it. Would it be uncomfortable at first? She wondered if...

Bailey leaned close to her ear. "That was a good one."

"Y-Yes, it was." Ava wanted her to say something else, for those lips to brush against her ear once more.

"How about we beat the crowd out of here?"

"Good idea." She bit her lip to hide a smile.

Like every other date, Bailey walked Ava to her front door and hugged her close. She was so tall, Ava's head stopped at her shoulder. She tried not to cling to Bailey but she had a way of holding her just right, making her feel that was the safest spot in the world. The hug didn't last long enough but Ava made sure her lips brushed against Bailey's neck as she pulled away. She felt the slight jerk of her body but Bailey's face didn't hold a hint of reaction. Ava locked the door behind her and pouted. Maybe Bailey didn't want her. Maybe she changed her mind.

Bailey waited for the click of the lock and exhaled. Those silky lips found the right spot and it took every ounce of resolve not to back Ava up against her front door. *Shit*. This was harder than she thought. She slowly walked back to her car looking back every so often in case Ava changed her mind. *Damn*. The flesh on her neck still tingled from the touch of those lips. Those full, sensual lips. Bailey sat in the car another twenty minutes before pulling off toward home. What was taking her so long? She could count at least six women who gave it up quicker than Ava. Bailey threw her keys on the kitchen counter, grabbed a beer and sat in her recliner. She surfed the channels and settled on a classic rerun when her cell phone rang. *Ava*.

"Hello?" Bailey took a swig of her beer.

"Hey, I was just making sure you made it home okay." Ava lay across her bed, freshly showered.

"I did make it home okay." She replied. "Thanks for checking on me."

"No problem. I also wanted to tell you that I had a wonderful time tonight."

"So did I. But I always have a wonderful time with you." Ava blushed. "Aww, how sweet."

Bailey smiled. "What are you doing?"

"I'm laying across the bed."

"Really?"

"Yeah, I just got out the shower."

"Oh okay." She waited a few beats. "Let me know if you need any help applying lotion or anything."

Ava giggled. "Nice to know chivalry isn't dead. I do appreciate the offer."

"Just trying to be of service."

"One day I'll have to take you up on that." Ava's heart raced. "There are a few spots I can't reach."

"I can definitely help with unreachable spots." Bailey lowered her tone an octave.

"Mmm, I'm sure you could." She sighed. "I'm also sure it would be an enjoyable experience."

"Oh you do?" She chuckled. "What makes you think so?"

"Your training as a musician has taught you patience. Plus all that practice you put in flexing those fingers." Ava boldly replied. It was something about the phone that gave her more courage than she really had.

"I guess you have a point. You'll have to tell me if your assumptions are true. One day."

"Right. One day. I have a question."

"I might have an answer."

"What did you do with it?" Ava asked. She blushed at the thought of that decadent phallus.

"Right now, it's in my closet." Bailey replied smoothly. "Waiting."

She smiled. "What is it waiting for?"

Bailey chuckled. "To slide into you, Baby."

Ava throbbed from the aggressiveness. "Thanks for the warning."

"You know what, that is exactly what it is, too." was the smug reply.

Ava felt the flesh between her legs grow even hotter. "We might need to talk about something else."

"You brought it up." Bailey reminded her.

"I know but I didn't know what I was getting myself into." She swallowed against the image of Bailey fucking her with the strap-on.

"What have you gotten yourself into?" Bailey could hear the heavy breathing through the phone. "What did I do?"

"Nothing." Ava lied.

"Ava."

"What?"

"Did I get you wet?" Bailey asked, certain of the answer.

Ava shook her head at Bailey's perception. "Fuck yeah, you did."

Bailey settled back in her recliner. "How wet are you?"

Her breathe caught in her throat. "I'm pretty wet."

Smiling, Bailey said, "Did you feel or are you just telling me that?"

"No, I'm feeling right now." Ava kicked her panties from around her ankles. "My clit is swollen too. I'm going to have to take care of this later."

"Why not now?" Bailey asked. "Why can't I hear it?"

"Hear what? Hear me?" Ava's pussy twitched at the request.

"Yeah, hear you." Bailey's tone was sexy and reassuring. "It's just me."

"O-okay." Ava was suddenly self-conscious as she dipped her hand between her thighs. The silence on the other end of the phone was deafening. "Now I'm nervous."

"Don't be nervous." Bailey soothed. "Close your eyes."

Ava did as she was told, adjusting the Bluetooth headset. Her fingers glided across smooth skin leading to her wet pussy. Soft saxophone music filtered through to her ear. It was one of Bailey's songs. The melody was relaxing and Ava felt her body melt into the mattress.

"I wish I was there with you right now." Bailey murmured.

"Mmm. I wish you were too." Ava sighed. "You could have all the pussy you wanted."

"Oh really?"

"Mmm-hmm." Ava's legs inched apart. "As long as you make it feel good."

"Don't worry. I have plans for what I'm going to do to your pussy." Bailey was assuring.

"Oh you do? And what are your plans, Mr. Bailey?" Ava asked saucily. Her hand moved closer to her still throbbing clit.

"First, I will taste you."

"Shit." Fingertips brushed across moist, swollen flesh.

"I'm going to nibble and suck your clit between my lips."

"You are? I'd like that." Ava rotated her clit in a circular motion. "It is pretty sensitive."

"Oh, I will make it feel good. Your legs will be wrapped around my shoulders." Bailey informed her. "You'll have to keep them up for a long time."

Ava dipped between the folds of her labia. The wetness was trickling down the curves of her ass. "I can keep my legs up."

"Because my tongue will be inside you so deep and I need your legs up high for that."

"I can do it, Bailey. I can do it." Ava's heels dug into the mattress; her body covered in a thin sheen of perspiration.

"You better be able to do it. I'm going to eat your pussy, Baby, and I'm going to take my time."

"Oh shit. You are?" Her breaths were short and quick as her fingers continued their pursuit of satisfaction.

"I sure will. My tongue will taste every part of that sweet, wet pussy until I have enough."

"Mmm, fuck." Ava felt herself teetering on the brink. "I sure will let you."

"Oh, I know you will."

"How do you know?"

"I'll make you want it. You will beg me not to stop."

"Oh! Mmm."

"I'll feel your nails in the back of my head as I feast on your pussy. I'll catch you if you try to run from me."

"I might run." Ava's feet dug into the mattress.

"You'll try." Bailey was sitting up in the recliner. The sounds Ava was making was a sweet melody. "But I'll catch you every time you get away. If you get away."

"Fuck! Y-You w-will? Fuck, Bailey!"

Bailey smiled. "You trying to tell me something?"

"I-I…" The force of her pending release shook her body. "Ooooh."

"Talk to me, Baby. Tell me something."

"I'm c-c-cumming." Ava's reply was low and guttural.

"You cumming for me?"

"Yes!"

"I need to feel it on my cheeks, Ava. You better cum all over my face." Bailey demanded, standing up.

"I'm trying, Daddi! Fuck, I'm trying!" Ava couldn't hold it any longer. She clutched at the pillow next to her, biting into the cushion and riding the waves of her orgasm. "Oh fuck, oh fuck."

Bailey waited until the tide ebbed. "Are you okay, Baby?"

"Mmm. Oh my goodness." Ava blushed. "I can't believe I just…damn."

Bailey chuckled. "What's wrong?"

"Nothing. But I suggest you get over here to finish what you started."

CHAPTER 8

Bailey arrived on Ava's doorstep within a half hour. Ava greeted her shyly, a little embarrassed after what took place on the phone. Bailey smiled back but didn't give her time to think and backed her against the nearest wall. Ava tugged at Bailey's thin t-shirt, running her hands over her breasts.

"Where's the couch?" Bailey demanded, pushing Ava's lounge pants past her hips.

"We are n-not..."

"Okay, okay. Where's the bed, Ava?"

"Down the hall." Ava pulled her toward the bedroom, holding up her pants with the other hand. "I can't believe you came over."

"You told me to." Bailey kissed her again, moving her hands across ample breasts and perky nipples. She removed Ava's camisole, placing soft kisses down her neck and collarbone.

"Shit. I know I told you to but I just didn't think..." Ava grabbed her shoulders when Bailey continued kissing down her chest, a wet tongue flicking across her nipple.

"You think too much." She backed Ava into the room until they collided with the bed. The pants tangled around Ava's legs and she quickly kicked her feet free.

Ava shuddered as Bailey's hands smoothed down her bare hips and thighs. Her mouth teased Ava's nipples to erection, then through the valley between her breasts, and across the soft skin of her stomach. Her lips fluttered across her moist center, buckling Ava's knees and she collapsed to the bed. Bailey stripped the rest of her own clothes, the discarded articles landing in a heap on the floor. Then she captured Ava's legs, her lips teasing the inside of thighs and the skin between legs and pussy. Ava squirmed, lifting her hips toward Bailey's mouth, silently begging for an end to the torture.

"Be patient." Bailey instructed.

"Are you serious?" was the raspy reply.

"Very." Her lips scalded Ava again, causing a fierce shudder.

"Shit. Bailey."

"I love the way you same my name." Bailey slid her tongue across pouty labia and inside velvet warmth. Muscles tightened around her tongue as Ava's hips bucked again.

"Oh my ... shit."

Bailey chuckled and withdrew her tongue, gliding around Ava's swollen clit. Her hands pulled her closer. Bailey stopped teasing and sucked the plump morsel between her lips. The heat from her mouth unsettled Ava, her mind teetered between consciousness and floating on the wave of pleasure. The heels of Ava's feet dug into her lower back. Bailey's tongue dipped again, taunting Ava until she scooted backwards.

"Where are you going?"

"Play fair, Baby."

"Where's the fun in that?" Her tongue thrust home again.

Ava shuddered and gripped the sheets. The tension spread throughout her body as Bailey feasted. The exhilaration forced her to back up a few times, only to be caught again. Her moans grew louder with each swirl of Bailey's tongue. She accepted defeat, realizing that the mini orgasms were robbing her energy. Ava pushed against Bailey's head which wasn't an effective deterrent. Bailey continued her pursuit, ignoring her feeble attempts. Ava's body warmed and her chest grew tighter; nipples chilled from the cool air in the room. She couldn't hold it and her hips lifted from the bed as forceful waves of ecstasy rolled within her body.

"Bailey! Oh fuck! Wait a m-minute."

Bailey gripped her thighs tighter, continued her torment until Ava collapsed. Her breathing was heavy and legs slack. Bailey smiled, obviously pleased with the results and inched up Ava's body. Ava grabbed her greedily, wrapping her arms around Bailey's shoulders and kissed her. Bailey positioned herself between Ava's legs and it was then Ava felt the firm, phallic object.

Her eyes flew open. "Are you wearing...?"

Bailey kissed down Ava's neck and collarbone. "Just relax."

Ava held her breath as Bailey pushed inside, stretching and filling her completely. Bailey waited a few beats and then withdrew partially, moving back in a second later. She continued until Ava joined the easy rhythm, her hips falling in sync. Bailey deliberately increased to a rapid pace. Ava wrapped her ankles around Bailey's calves and caught up with the new tempo. She knew she was close again and involuntarily gripped Bailey's back tighter, legs tensing.

"Not yet." Bailey commanded, pulling out. She turned Ava over to her stomach, pulled her up to her knees and entered her again.

"Oh shit!" Ava buried her face into the sheets to muffle the screams from her neighbors. There was something very erotic about Bailey's hands on the small of her back and hips, and all she could do was take it. Ava let Bailey guide her into another rhythm but couldn't match her speed. Then it felt too good and she needed a minute to collect her passion. She tried to scoot away.

"Where're you going?" Bailey eased into a slow rotation.

"Mmm, Baby. I need..." Ava's hips had a mind of their own, matching each of Bailey's swirls.

"What do you need, Ava?" She reached around to stroke her clit.

"Are you kidding me? That's not f-fair." She clawed at the sheets again and knew she couldn't hold this one. It had gained momentum and threatened to not only spill over but explode. "I'm..."

Bailey felt the unmistakable shudder overtake Ava's body, before her knees crumpled from beneath her. She smiled and pulled out. Releasing the harness, Bailey wiggled out and stretched out beside a snoozing Ava, drawing her in an embrace. She kissed her shoulders.

Ava scooted away. "Uh uh. I can't...too sleepy."

Bailey snickered and pulled her back. "I'm not starting anything. Go back to sleep."

"You better not be." She replied, drifting off again.

CHAPTER 9

va opened her eyes, stretched languidly and smiled at the sore spots. Blushing, she remembered the position that caused the tenderness. A soft snore on the other side of the bed deepened her blush and she slipped from underneath the sheets. Ava tied her hair up in a scarf and shower cap. Standing underneath a cascade of warm water, she washed places where Bailey's lips and hands incited her lustful appetite. Bailey exceeded Ava's expectations by showing a sensitive side. Those strong arms that bent her into submission also cradled her as she slept. What surprised Ava most was that she disregarded a rule. Her emotions got the best of her – again. She blamed it on the music for weakening her resolve and tickling her libido. *Now what?* The morning after was always the hardest. Ava didn't want to expect too much too soon. It had only been a month. She shook her head. One month. One awesome month.

Bailey was tying her shoes when Ava stepped out of the bathroom. She steeled for a negative reaction and a famous exit line. Instead, Bailey smiled at Ava, making her blush again.

"You wouldn't happen to have an extra toothbrush, do you?" She asked.

"Um, no."

"I didn't think so and of course, I did forget to bring one."

Ava giggled. "Yeah, I guess you did."

Bailey moved toward her and Ava's breath lodged in her throat. Her pussy instantly tingled in anticipation. "You have class in a couple of hours, right?"

"You remembered."

"Why wouldn't I?" She gave Ava a peck on the forehead and a long hug. "I should get going so I can grab a shower before rehearsal."

"Okay."

"But I'll see you later tonight, though." Bailey squeezed her again before letting go.

"Tonight?"

"Yeah, you know at that place we call work."

Ava's sunshine day dulled a bit. She'd forgotten about work.

Rumors Ring True

Episode Two:
It's Complicated

CHAPTER ONE

The buzzing of the alarm clock creeped into Cole's slumber and cajoled her awake. She opened her eyes slowly, aware of the extra set of lungs on the other side of the fold-out bed. Her bare feet connected with the floor and she stretched to clear out some more cobwebs. The morning's bright rays streamed in through the mini-blinds of her office window. Cole stumbled in the bathroom for a quick shower to wash away last night's scotch and sex. Smelling fresh, she emerged in boxer briefs, sports bra and an a-shirt. The curvaceous beauty turned over to her stomach, letting the sheet slip down to expose naked skin. Cole shook her head and picked a tailored, chocolate colored suit with matching tie, and a cream shirt. The woman still hadn't stirred by the time Cole slipped on the chocolate and cream Stacy Adams. She heard some of the staff already moving around the restaurant.

"Daphne!" Cole stood over the sleeping form, adjusting her custom cufflinks. "You need to get up."

Daphne lifted her tousled head, makeup smeared across her eyes. "You know just once I wish you'd fuck me and treat me nice afterwards."

Cole ignored the remark and pulled chocolate suspenders over her shoulders. "I need to get to work."

Daphne sighed, knowing she wouldn't win the argument. Gracefully, she slid from the bed and stretched. Cole admired her svelte form and full breasts. Daphne was a good lay, always eager to please but naively believed she could change wandering ways.

"Push the bed back in, will you?"

Cole locked the door to the office, traveling down the hallway toward the kitchen and morning shift preparations. Tasha bellowed orders to the various prep cooks and smirked at Cole when she passed by. After making sure all employees were where they needed to be, she returned to the office. Daphne finished arranging the pillows on the couch.

"When's the last time you changed these sheets?" She asked.

"Since the last time we fucked." Cole replied.

Daphne pretended to straighten her tie. "Whatever. I know I'm not the only heifer in your harem."

Cole stepped around Daphne. "I don't recall us being exclusive."

"Don't remind me."

"I need to get my restaurant open."

Daphne recognized the dismissal. "Of course, will you call me later?"

"If I'm not busy."

"Ok." She opened the door.

"Daphne…" Cole began.

"Don't worry." Daphne interrupted. "I'm going out the back door."

Cole waited until she heard the door close before exhaling. Daphne would never understand why she wasn't the one. Cole supposed she had too much of her Aunt Maxi in her. Maxi's affections ran cold rather quickly even though she was ever at a loss for female companionship. She'd rather romance a lonely housewife with no strings attached. This produced plenty of jealous lovers, angry husbands and a few public tirades. Cole nipped that behavior in the bud by stating her intentions up front. She didn't have time for a bunch of nonsense and drama when she had a restaurant to run.

Margie, Cole's mother, described her older sister as a free spirit often hinting that she took after Maxi a little too much. Maxi toured with a Jazz band for most of her youth as first trumpet and usually had a willing beauty waiting at the next gig. Whenever she stopped through on her way somewhere else, Cole ate up the stories of life on the road and her many flirtations. Life as a single parent left Margie with little to no extra time and Aunt Maxi was happy to fill in the gaps when she could. She encouraged Cole's interest in the trombone, paying for lessons and attending every recital and band competition when she was home.

After accumulating a hefty nest egg, Maxi retired and opened her club. The word spread that Maxi had friends in high places who liked to stop by, reminisce about old times and take in a few shows. The local talent started begging for stage time and the club took off from there. Maxi kept her dreadlocks trimmed around her hairline, very low key with one sapphire pinkie ring and a silver necklace with a treble clef pendant. She dressed in the best men's fashions and could work a crowd. Sauntering through a thick mob of patrons, Maxi delivered a smooth smile with a firm handshake. Cole spent a lot of time at the club, under the watchful eye of her aunt. Maxi let Cole's garage trio play at the club a few times and gave her a job. She bussed tables for two years until she was eighteen and became a bar back.

Maxi made it known that she was grooming her niece to take over the club. Cole sat in on business meetings concerning the club, in awe of how her aunt's mind worked. She leaned back in her chair, puffed on a handcrafted, briarwood pipe and left her victim fidgeting in silence. Cole wanted the business but her feet itched to see the world too. She promised her mother she would graduate college before she set out on her own. Aunt Maxi didn't object and spurred on Cole's wanderlust. She had just graduated when her plans were waylaid and then no longer considered the day Maxi was diagnosed with throat cancer. Her aunt fought it bravely with an aggressive treatment schedule.

When her treatments zapped all the energy out of Maxi, Cole took over managing the club. She dug deep and realized her own dreams didn't matter when it came to being there for what little family she had. Cole and Margie sat at her bedside, trying to keep up lively conversation as Maxi endured the pain. Her death hit them hard, catapulting both into a short depression. Margie lost her sister and best friend. Cole lost an aunt, a mentor and the only father she ever knew. She closed the restaurant for two weeks, locking herself away at home. Cole played all of Maxi's records over and over. She didn't sleep, couldn't eat and refused any attempts of consolation until Margie put her foot down.

"You made her a promise, Colette." Margie's eyes flashed. "And you better keep it. She loved you too much to want you doing this to yourself."

The day the club reopened, Cole poured all of her efforts into Maxi's Place by revamping the spot and introduced an appetizer menu. The appetizers were such a hit she hired a chef for some specialized entrées and added a host stand. Cole continued the tradition of local entertainment, designing a VIP section for the now famous artists Maxi helped along the way. They always stopped through to show respect for the woman who gave them a chance and possibly an impromptu performance. Business boomed and space was limited so Cole purchased the empty buildings on either side. She added a full service kitchen and renovated the bathrooms. The stage was enlarged to allow more space for entertainment.

Expansion took four months but the results paid off. Mondays and Tuesdays were open by reservation only, usually for businesses or private functions. Karaoke night on Wednesdays was a cult hit for the customers as well as the employees. Thursdays was Ladies' Night with specials on wine and fruity concoctions. They had a loyal crowd at the end of the week thanks to Cole's promotional efforts. Friday happy hour promised a packed house and the night would be humping from eight until closing at one a.m. Saturday was for the dinner crowd but the restaurant opened early for Sunday brunch.

Each day had its own routine but Friday was their busiest day. Cole briefed her security team, checked the reservation book at the host stand and the stock at the bar. She headed backstage to confirm the talent and tie up free time between acts. By the time Cole stepped into the kitchen, Tasha had her cooks jumping at every bark.

"The iron fist strikes hard." Cole smiled at her jump.

"Stopping sneaking up on me." Tasha's look shot daggers. "What do you want anyway?"

"Just checking on the kitchen."

"This is one part of the restaurant you don't have to worry about." She smirked.

"Now you know that I worry about every part of my business." Cole replied. "It's the plight of an owner."

"So you say. I think you need a vacation." Her eyes glinted. "Or at least try sleeping alone so you can get some rest."

"There is no fun in sleeping alone, Tasha. Not everyone is in a committed relationship."

"You have to want to be in one."

Cole chuckled. "You got me there."

Tasha shook her head. "You still refuse to change, huh?"

"Why is this such a serious conversation all of a sudden?" She asked, with a crooked grin. "We have three hours until happy hour and we're talking about change. How about we talk about the reservation book?"

Tasha sighed. There was no use pushing the matter. "Any recent surprises?"

"A couple of six tops changed to eight"

"Okay, nothing I can't handle."

"That's why you're the chef."

This Friday was busier than the last and Cole was glad she staffed an extra hostess. The waiting area and bar were so thick with people Cole had to wiggle her way to the host stand. Usually a night like this produced some drunken foolishness. Daniel poured sugar on the impatient throng and appeased the most upset ones with free appetizer cards.

"How many names on the wait, Daniel?" Cole asked, smiling at the guest in line.

"Only about twenty-five or so. I just sat four tables." He answered, self-assured in his hosting capabilities.

"Good." There was never a complaint from the guests when Daniel worked. The employees were a completely different subject. Daniel listened too hard, talked too much and abused his position. He was also the best lead host until Ava came along. The power struggle was obvious every time they worked together – which was every Friday night.

"However, I do need to visit the little girl's room."

"Where's Ava?"

Daniel smirked. "Seating a guest."

"Hurry back." Cole turned back to the wait list. "How many in your party?"

"Two." Her light eyes were obvious contact lenses but she at least found a color which suited her caramel skin. A maroon blouse dipped low, showcasing voluptuous cleavage.

She smiled. "Your name?"

"Monique."

Cole handed her a pager. "Right now we're on a thirty to forty-five minute wait."

"I heard it's worth it." She pulled the tall, lanky woman next to her into the crowd. Monique looked back and smiled at Cole again before disappearing.

When Ava returned, Cole let her take over with instructions about the wait list and pushed through the herd to the bar. Her lead bartender, Logan, was hard at work smooth-talking a pretty coed. Logan could make any type of drink. Whenever a customer sauntered up to the bar, in search of a liquid to help release inhibitions, Logan would ask them a few questions and then present them with refreshment completely right for the moment. Shots were her specialty and the biggest reason Cole hired her. Logan could give you a Royal Fuck or some Buttery Nipples. How about a Honey Dew Me and a few Screaming Orgasms? Looking for more of a cocktail, these days it was Apple Martinis for the ladies, Hennessy Neat for the gents.

Tall and athletic, Logan worked out religiously. Her toned biceps shook the coldest martinis and filled in as a bouncer if necessary. Most of her regulars were Femmes who loved to smooth their hands across her muscles and stare into those caramel, brown eyes. Logan flashed those pearly whites, passed out a few winks and pocketed their phone numbers. However, she was a hard worker and knew how to whip a green bartender into shape.

"Boss Lady, how're things tonight?" Logan grabbed a towel to wipe the bar.

"Good. How is it back here?" Cole scanned the patrons perched on barstools.

"Doing good, raking it in. A lot of cuties out tonight." She grinned.

"I don't care how many numbers you get, remember you're at work." Cole caught the eye of Monique at the end of the bar. That bouncing bosom was mouthwatering but would have to wait. She had a restaurant to run.

CHAPTER TWO

Bailey peeked out from behind the stage curtain. The usual butterflies invaded her stomach but she wasn't concerned with the crowd as she searched for Ava. This was a habit she picked up for the past three months. Their shared secret was exciting at first. It even caused a few steamy nights after work. Ava wasn't like other women Bailey dated and she silently admitted she was a little intimidating. Bailey assumed Ava would crowd her at some point. Most of her ex's became clingy after sex but Ava's independence was a surprise. Her goals and ambition were a turn on and Bailey only thought of Ava when she had an itch.

Smart, funny, and responsible, Ava was at the other end of Bailey's spectrum. Urges to just be in her presence were overwhelming and more than a little unsettling. She refused to admit she hated the secrecy and was a little unsure of how to handle the foreign emotion of jealousy. An unknown angst always pricked her heart whenever Bailey analyzed Ava's motives for their clandestine affair. No one knew about it. No one at work. None of their friends.

Bailey played that game before and only for one reason – for crushing on another chick.

Ava appeared with a large party following her to a table adorned with birthday decorations. Even in the drab, black uniform, she saw Ava's sexy curves. A few hours ago, Bailey was in between those soft thighs, grinding her cares away. As if she knew Bailey was standing there, Ava glanced at the stage while rushing back to the host stand. Heat spread through her chest and down to her loins. Sighing, Bailey moved away from the curtain and checked her sax one more time. That woman fucked with her head. She took a deep breath, stretched her neck and said a quick meditation. Lost in her happy place, Bailey didn't hear Cole walk up until she was standing next to her.

"Two minutes, Bailey." Cole shook her hand. "How're the chops tonight?"

"Fantastic, Boss Lady." She grinned. "I promise it will be quite a show."

"I have no doubt, son." Cole slapped her on the back, adjusted her cuff links and stepped through the curtain. She waved at a few patrons and grabbed a microphone off the baby grand piano. Cole slipped a hand into her pants pocket and produced an easy grin she was famous for.

"Ladies and gentlemen, welcome to Maxi's Place. I'm Cole Washington." She took a practiced step backwards to wait for the claps and whistles to die down. "Thank you. Y'all are the best. As always, I appreciate you joining my family this evening. You could have gone anywhere tonight but you chose to come here. I'm very grateful for all of the love but I know who you really came to see tonight. *Thompson 5!*" Cole nodded at the ensuing roar. "Now I want everyone to have a great time tonight. However, I will caution the ladies to refrain from throwing your panties on stage this evening." She pointed at a few regulars in the crowd, drawing laughter and intoxicated giggles from the revelers. "Be sure to ask your server about the drink specials. I won't hold up the show any longer. Their CD is due out later this year and I assure you, it's one you need to add to your collection. Give a Maxi's Place welcome to a group of five family members who have developed quite a following. *Thompson 5!*"

The applause was deafening as Cole retreated behind the curtain until the quintet began its first set. Then she circled the restaurant again. She checked the host stand, bar and traveled through the kitchen before swinging through the VIP section. Daniel seated them in one of the booths along the wall. The dark brown leather was comfortable and private with high backed seats. Cole introduced herself to the pair.

"I know who you are." Monique replied. "Everyone does."

Cole slid in next to her. "I don't care about everyone else."

Monique smiled. "You're smooth."

"In so many ways." She licked her lips. "Look I have to get back to work. Don't worry about your tab."

Cole returned a few more times. Each encounter, Monique greeted her with sexual innuendoes and flirty expressions. She noticed a hint of a slur and the absence of food on the table. The perfectly coiffed face began to slacken a little and even with the colorful contacts, a glaze was slowly creeping into her eyes. By the end of the set, Cole changed her mind and already had a plan of escape. She returned to VIP for a last visit and found Monique slumped to the side of the booth. Cole waited for her to recognize that an extra person was sitting there.

"Girl, you snuck up on me!" She playfully pushed Cole's shoulder.

"My apologies. How are you feeling?"

"I'm feeling a bit thirsty." Monique reached over and squeezed her thigh, making sure her breasts brushed against her arm. She leaned into Cole, taking a healthy nip at her ear. "Ain't nobody got head game like Mo. Best believe that."

The alcoholic fumes burned her nose and she faked a smile. "Oh really?"

"Mmmhmm. Need references?" Her shoulders shook and a sotted screech escaped.

"I don't think I do." Cole stood. "I need to get back to work though."

"Hurry back, Daddi."

"As soon as I can." She stopped the drink delivery and changed the order. Only food would soak up some of that alcohol. What a disappointment. "Logan, print me the ticket for table three in VIP."

"Sure Boss Lady." Logan handed it to her.

"Thanks." Cole scanned the many expensive drinks. Not one thing to eat. She stopped Daniel on his way back to the host stand. "Call a cab for VIP table three."

"Didn't go as planned, Boss Lady?"

"Call the fucking cab."

He pouted. "Okay, okay."

Cole shoved the ticket in her pocket. One day she'd learn that some women weren't used to particular things in life and took advantage of certain situations. Cole found the kitchen still humming. They switched to a limited appetizer menu after eleven and Tasha started the eventual shutdown at 1 a.m. She never missed a step in running her sous chefs or the kitchen.

"Too late for a sandwich?" Cole asked.

"No, I think we can rustle something up." Tasha replied, without looking up from her clipboard. "Had a change of plans, huh?"

She sighed. "My private life seems to be a popular topic."

"You shouldn't make your private life so public." Tasha retorted.

Cole shook her head. "Can't depend on a drunken woman."

She chuckled. "So true. What do you want on your sandwich?"

"The usual."

"How do you know I have bacon right now?"

"I have faith that you do." Cole nudged Tasha with her shoulder. "Appreciate it."

Tasha watched her leave, biting back a remark. Of course she had bacon but that wasn't the point. Tasha returned to her inventory, staying conscious of the time. Two hours would pass before Cole retreated to that office to count the night's receipts. That's when she would want that damn sandwich she loved so much.

Tasha waited until she knew Cole was sitting at her desk with a highball of scotch before bringing her sandwich. This was the only time of night the machine seemed human. Dedicated and ambitious, she spent hours thinking about how Maxi's Place could be better. Tasha was her sounding board and often called upon to give an opinion about one scheme or another. She didn't mind watching Cole's brain do it's magic. Now if only her sexy ass wasn't such a womanizer, she would be a half decent Stud.

Cole was down to rolled up shirt sleeves with her suspenders pulled off her shoulders and left to dangle around her hips. Her tie was missing as well, more than likely hanging next to the matching suit coat. The highball sat on a coaster on the desk. Tired eyes and a smile greeted her as she walked in.

"You are a lifesaver." She stood and met Tasha halfway. "I'm starving."

"Did you eat today?"

"Here and there."

"That means no." Tasha glanced at the sleeper and decided against sitting on it. "You need to take care of your body, Cole."

"Are you submitting an application?" She asked.

"Just mannish."

Cole grinned between chews and swallowed. "Thanks for the sandwich. Awesome as always."

"You know I do have other recipes."

"I remember the first time you made me this sandwich."

Tasha started. "Cole…"

"We fucked for hours that day." She remarked. "I was starving then too."

Tasha shook her head. "Why bring that up?"

"I had a memory."

"Whatever."

"What?" Cole took another bite.

"You love to bring that up just to get a reaction out of me." She told her. "I think that's the real reason you ask for that damn sandwich."

"Does your stubby know about us?"

Tasha sighed at the shift in conversation. Typical Cole. "What does she have to do with what we're talking about right now?"

"So that's a no." She raised her eyebrows.

"I wouldn't hear the end of it if she knew. She'd either be here every night or up my ass to quit."

"Fuck her. You were the chef here long before you met her lazy ass."

"Why are we talking about her?"

"I wondered if she knew." Cole shrugged her shoulders and took a sip of scotch.

"I bet you did." Tasha rolled her eyes. "I'm not sure why you care. You have your hands full."

"Do I hear the beginning of a lecture?"

"No, I don't have time for that. I need to get back to work." She stalked out the door.

CHAPTER THREE

The luminescent hands on the wall clock announced 3:07 a.m. when Logan turned the key to her studio apartment. She kicked her slip resistant shoes off and emptied her pockets on the table next to the door. Several business cards and scraps of paper formed a small, messy mountain of phone numbers. They would eventually find a home in the trash can. Logan trudged across the wood floor to the bathroom and emerged a short time later free of the sour alcoholic stench clinging to her skin. She rustled up a turkey sandwich on wheat bread, complete with lettuce, tomatoes and a few jalapeños. Popping open a frosty beer, she checked her email, played on a social network and surfed some websites. Logan knew she should be counting sheep at this point but falling asleep was a difficulty lately. She quickly grew bored and grabbed her weights.

Weight lifting was more than stress relief or healthy living. This was the only time Logan's brain stopped going a mile a minute. With each curl she counted backwards from fifteen, squeezing her biceps at precisely the right moment. Next Logan punished her triceps, holding one dumbbell above her head and pressed upwards. She didn't stop until the burn was unbearable and her arms stopped cooperating. Logan took a fifteen second breather and then dropped to the floor for some push-ups. She lost count but kept going until her arms collapsed beneath her. Gasping for air, the tell-tale signs of exhaustion finally set in and she rolled off the floor to collapse in the bed a few feet away.

Peace happened with unexpected swiftness and Logan soon floated beyond time when life wasn't so complicated. A crisp, cool morning filled her lungs and exited in a foggy cloud. The sun peeked over the orange horizon casting purple and yellow streaks across the sky. The grass, still moist with dew, held a fresh cut smell from yesterday afternoon. Logan could feel the wetness through her maroon sweatpants as she reached for the toes of her maroon and gold track shoes. She enjoyed the air moving over her bare arms and the ensuing goosebumps. Her fellow student athletes were clad in their matching hoodies. *Except her.* She loved morning just as much as Logan. She didn't bother with sweats either, preferring thin running shorts instead. Her stretching routine, practiced and flawless, mesmerized quite a few raging hormones. Logan wasn't immune to her feminine wiles and stopped mid-stretch when she spread her legs, bending at the waist to stretch her hamstrings. Logan remembered where she was and quickly looked away before she was caught revealing a secret. Those secret feelings she wasn't supposed to have. Logan stood and ran in place for a couple of seconds, gazing far down the practice field. Then she was right in front of her, a playful smirk on those full lips and a gleam in her hazel eyes.

"May I run with you, Logan?" Her voice was sweet and lilting, landing softly on the eardrums.

Logan didn't know she knew her name. "Sure."

"Good." She punched Logan in the arm. "Hope you can keep up."

Logan awoke with a start, heart pounding and confused. She sat up and tried to rub the memory from her eyes. She could smell the perfume in the air and her body defiantly reacted. The flesh between her thighs twitched, growing moist as her clit hardened. It was taking longer than usual for the vision to disappear and Logan fled to the shower to cool off. The fragrance seemed embedded in her skin and it wouldn't scrub off. Wore out, she gave up and sat down in the tub, letting the water spray cascade over her head. The throbbing intensified and Logan slid her fingers across her drenched body. Hazel eyes danced laughingly while she gently stroked. *I hope you can keep up.* Silky lips brushed her neck. Brazen hands held her close. Teeth nipped at her ears and Logan bit back a deep moan. Her juices mixed with the water swirling around her ass and hips. After some long minutes, she turned off the water. Shame overwhelmed her as she dried off her steaming skin and slipped into some boxer briefs. Logan lay down gingerly, nervous about closing her eyes. The sun was peeking over the horizon when she drifted to sleep.

CHAPTER FOUR

Tasha stopped at the doorframe of Cole's office. The room reeked of that horrid cigar she was so fond of. Her tie was missing and the opened collar displayed her favorite silver, labrys necklace, catching the glare from the lamp as it swung to and fro. The sleeves were rolled up to her elbows and a glass of scotch was in easy reach. She tapped furiously at an electronic calculator, an endless ribbon of white paper forming a pile on her desk. She was always working.

"I'm ready." Tasha stopped in the middle of the room.

Cole glanced up, wrote down a figure and stood to stretch. "Great job tonight, Sha Sha."

She shrugged. "It's what I do."

"Still can't take a compliment."

"Sorry." Tasha smiled at the teasing. "Thank you, Cole."

"You're very welcome." She sauntered around the desk. Tasha didn't move as she came closer. "And you still look sexy."

"Whatever." Tasha turned to walk out, leaving Cole to follow her.

She never could open this back door and tonight was no exception. Tasha pushed hard but it didn't cooperate. She bounced off and landed against Cole, who grabbed her hips to steady her. For a few seconds, Tasha's ass was settled against Cole's front.

Tasha pulled away. "D-Damn door. I thought you were going to get this fixed, Cole."

"You're the only one having problems with the door, Sha Sha." She grinned. "Maybe I should show you how – again."

"Just open the fucking door."

Cole pushed it open with ease. "You know, you could stick around."

"N-No, I can't. Goodnight."

Cole watched Tasha walk the few feet to her car and drive off. She waved at the security guard before locking the door. She checked all the other doors one more time before returning to her office. She hated this time of night when even the angry beeps of car horns died down and the silence was deafening after all the noise of the evening. Cole turned on some Hip Hop music and picked up her drink. She took a few sips, letting the scotch burn down her throat. Laziness kept her from traveling the forty-five minute trek home. Sleeping on the fold-out bed was easier. However, it didn't mean that she had to sleep alone. Daphne answered on the third ring, voice thick with sleep.

"Have I been brought up from the back burner?"

"So we're a little salty, huh?"

Daphne was quiet. "You know, I shouldn't come over."

"It's your decision." Cole took another sip. "I just extended an invite."

"I didn't hear you ask me."

"No, you didn't. Before I could say hello, you said something rude."

"You're right. I'm sorry." She fell silent, waiting for the question.

Cole paused a few beats. "Daphne, would you like to come over?"

"To your house?"

"No, I'm at the restaurant."

"Oh." The disappointment was obvious. "I'll call when I'm in the parking lot."

"See you in a bit."

Cole finished her accounting and straightened up her desk. After a speedy shower, she switched to some sensual music and lit a scattering of candles. As she poured a glass of Moscato, her cell phone rang Daphne's arrival. Cole immediately turned on the charm. She flirted and paid Daphne the attention she was bugging her about. Neither was oblivious to the real reason why Cole called her in the wee hours. Even so, if Cole wanted to fulfill a fantasy, Daphne willingly played along. It took exactly two glasses of moscato to cause Daphne to loosen an inhibition that was far from prudish. An aggressive glint peeked around her eyes as she straddled Cole on the couch.

"I didn't wear panties." She purred. "Just like you like it."

Cole grinned, pushed the dress up and ran her knuckles across her flat stomach. Daphne let out a short moan and finished pulling the dress over her head. Her breasts were perky with chocolate nipples, standing at attention. She arched, allowing Cole's lips better access. Cole roughly caressed her curvaceous body, gliding her hands down the small dip of her back to the crest of her ass. Her hands returned to palm Daphne's breasts, gently kneading and fondling

"Please, Cole."

She brushed past an engorged clit and two fingers entered torrid wetness in one graceful stroke. "Is that what you wanted?"

"You know it is." Daphne rocked back and forth, a thin sheen of sweat beginning to coat her brow. Eyes closed, she was lost in her imagination. In another world, Cole came home, with a tender-worded greeting and made love to her.

~~~~~

A steaming bubble bath, her fuzzy pink sleep pants and a grilled cheese sandwich called out to Tasha the second she turned on her street. By habit, she scanned the front of her house for Kai's emerald green coupe. Not in its usual parking spot, Tasha briefly wondered where she was this evening. Strip club? Basketball gym? On someone's couch playing video games? She could be anywhere doing anything unless it was working. Kai was forever trying to find herself. No one knew if she ever would. After two years, Tasha was out of suggestions and gave up being supportive of the next fast money-making scheme. They all required the one ingredient that Kai wasn't willing to provide - hard work.

With no extra time to languish in a tub, Tasha opted for a shower instead. Relaxation was fleeting and she was wound up more than usual tonight. The kitchen always gave her an adrenaline high and it took hours to float down from that rush. There was nothing more satisfying than creating works of edible art. Cooking was all she ever wanted to do. Her grandmother smiled when Tasha went to culinary school but warned that they will only teach the basics. *Cooking comes from the heart.* Grandmama was right and Tasha spent hours in a hot kitchen perfecting her craft. She worked hard on the menus, scheduling, inventory and whatever else needed to be done. All because Cole gave her a chance and believed in her vision. *Cole.*

Tasha sat at the island counter and wished for the tenth time today that she hadn't stopped smoking. She poured a glass of chardonnay to combat the restless feeling. She knew it wasn't Kai she was concerned about. Although she was between jobs once again, she at least picked up gigs as a personal trainer. Kai only had six steady clients but they were naïve and bought the exercise supplements she peddled. She was so different from Cole. *Cole.* That woman was on Tasha's mind a lot lately. More than what it should be. Something as simple as bacon, lettuce and tomato sandwiches had her mind conjuring flashbacks to an ice storm and three days of soulful lovemaking. Their relationship was best when they were lying down or up against something. Tasha fought a sudden throbbing and cursed her body's disloyalty.

The scratch of metal alerted Kai's arrival and moments later she heard the squeak of her basketball shoes on the tile floor. Kai may have been broke most of the time but she did manage to stay up to date with all the trends. Her shorts and jersey matched her hat – advertising the most popular professional basketball team. Her shoes matched the black and red ensemble perfectly. A smooth grin on her attractive features, she greeted Tasha with kiss on the cheek and slap on the ass. The unmistakable, pungent odor of weed and sweat wafted over her and Tasha was instantly irritated. So it had been the basketball court and hours of getting stoned.

"How was your night, sexy?" Kai pulled a beer out of the fridge.

"Busy." She replied coolly.

Kai picked up on the hostility. "Aw baby, I'm sorry you beat me home. I got caught up in some construction traffic."

Tasha refilled her wine glass. There was freeway construction all over the metroplex right now so Kai's excuse was believable but used often. This wasn't the first time she beat Kai home and usually they had an argument followed by some lustful, makeup sex. Tasha didn't feel like arguing. She needed to unwind and there was one thing that Kai worked hard at.

"Are you getting in the shower?"

Kai grinned. "Hopping in right now."

"I'll be waiting when you get out."

"You won't be waiting long." Kai kissed Tasha's neck as she passed, sliding her hand up to cup her breasts. She ran up the stairs in her usual stomping fashion.

Tasha sighed and took a gulp of wine. Cole used to kiss that same delicate spot. Such a simple contact caused her to lose restraint and they'd fuck wherever they were in the house at the moment. Kai's kisses felt a bit different and too wet. Tasha knew it didn't do any good comparing them. There was too much contrast. She refilled her glass, checked the front door and then climbed the stairs to the bedroom. She decided to make it easy on Kai and undressed. Tasha was laying in bed when she emerged from the bathroom, wearing white boxers. The sun tattoo around her belly button glistened from the baby oil she slathered across her skin.

"Damn, you said you'd be waiting." Kai jumped under the covers. "Did you miss me, baby?"

Tasha drained her wineglass. "Something like that."

CHAPTER FIVE

Ava didn't usually like bar and grills but made an exception for Bailey. The rowdy atmosphere was certainly entertaining. Hordes of baseball fans in their favorite team jerseys enjoyed beer, hot wings and trash talking. Ava laughed at the boisterous fan wearing red and blue face paint who kept trying to dance on the bar top. The hostesses and the two floor managers attempted to control the situation but every time they calmed him down, he waited a few minutes before trying to climb up on the bar again. Ava sent up a prayer of thanks for her job at Maxi's Place.

She scanned the crowd again for any familiar faces, a ritual performed every time she went out with Bailey. The bar and grill was on the other side of town from Maxi's Place but Ava had to make sure they wouldn't be found out. Tuesday nights was Bailey's practice night and it was either held at her brother Alvin's or sister's house. Tonight it was at Alvin's. She preordered a drink for Bailey, who always needed to blow off steam after a session with her siblings. It was a wonder they ever created music from all the bickering. Still a diehard fan, Ava wanted to attend a jam session but Bailey didn't trust their big mouths.

Three months sped by quickly after their first wild night together. Even though the sex was frequent, there were many nights where they just cuddled and talked. Ava didn't want to make any assumptions about their relationship status or rather their lack of one but under normal lesbian behavior they would have set a move-in date by now. If Bailey uttered those words of commitment, she would come running. She glanced at her cell phone, twirling the stem of her wine glass. Ava hoped she wasn't falling under the spell she was warned about. There was something about that stud. The obvious was Bailey had a sweet, sensitivity hiding behind bravado and cockiness. Although, Ava sensed an idiosyncrasy about her which she couldn't explain just yet. The tales of her past liaisons haunted Ava and she wasn't eager to become a statistic.

"Sorry I'm late." Bailey appeared and kissed her cheek. "Did you get my text?"

"Y-Yes, I did." Ava fought tremors. "How was practice?"

She grimaced. "I need a drink." The waitress appeared from amidst the ruckus and set a rum and coke in front of her. Bailey smiled at Ava before taking a healthy gulp. "You are a wonderful woman."

Ava shook her head. "Was it that bad?"

"It was worse." Bailey reached across the lacquered wooden table for her hand. "Alvin argued with Sheila the whole night. He said her beat was too fast. Monroe was late on every song and Denise was in a funk over a stupid boyfriend. I think we sounded a little flat."

"With all that going on, you probably were."

"Exactly." She winked. "How was your day, Beautiful?"

Ava blushed. "Full of classes and homework. I wanted to get it done and not have to worry about it later."

"So you're free for the evening?"

"Completely free."

"You know, I'm not really feeling hot wings anymore."

Quivers erupted on Ava's skin. "We could order in afterwards."

"Afterwards, huh?" Bailey grinned and signaled for the check. "Finish your drink."

She drained her glass and stood. "Race you to my place."

"I'll beat you there."

"Not with this head start."

In her giddy state, Ava paid no attention to the few stragglers in the parking lot. She took long strides to the car, her skin tingling from anticipation of Bailey's touch, her kisses, her...

"Ava?"

She froze in terror. There was no mistaking that voice. *Daniel.* She turned to the left and watched him sashay toward her. She glanced at the door. "Isn't this a small world?"

"Girl, what are you doing on this side of the universe?" Daniel smirked at her. "I don't think I've ever seen you over here before."

"A friend told me about the wings so I was grabbing a bite to eat." Ava replied. "So you were inside too?"

"No ma'am. I wouldn't be caught dead in the middle of that sports combat zone." He grimaced. "This diva can't do it."

Ava nodded and saw Bailey step out. She immediately looked around the parking lot. Daniel noticed her gaze and turned to be nosey.

"Well, this is certainly a small world." He remarked. "Do my eyes deceive me or is that Mr. Bailey walking this way?"

"The world is getting smaller by the minute." Ava came up with a quick story as Bailey approached. "I didn't even see her in there."

Bailey noticed Ava's expression and played along. "Funny seeing you two here."

Daniel searched Bailey's nonchalant attitude for a kink. "Well, I just happened to run into Ava and I thought what a coincidence. Then you appear and the hamsters start running a marathon. I can't help but wonder if I stumbled upon a romantic interlude."

"I told you I was here with friends, Daniel." Ava lied.

"Hmmm. Actually, you said you were grabbing a bite to eat at a friend's suggestion."

"Don't you have anything better to do?" Bailey moved closer. "You're always stirring up shit."

"I'm not stirring up shit. Why are you so defensive, Bailey Bear?"

"Hold on you two. This isn't necessary." Ava stepped between them. "It was nice running into you both. Goodnight."

"Goodnight girl." Daniel grinned. "Drive safely."

Bailey turned on her heel and stomped the few steps to her car. She counted to ten and turned the ignition. She wanted to cave Daniel's face in. The worst part was that he was right. They had been caught and forced to lie about it. Not that it was any of his business. Bailey knew Daniel would run to Cole with his newfound information and the consequences could be severe. Ava's call interrupted her manic thoughts.

"Are you alright?"

"Yeah, that motherfucker pisses me off."

Ava sighed. "I know a great way to work off some aggression."

Bailey loins twitched and she backed out of the parking space. "What way is that?"

"You'll see."

Ava pulled out in front of her and the race was on. This was a game they often played. The winner received no other reward except for bragging rights but for some reason the foreplay resulting from it was electric. Bailey followed close behind until they hit the freeway then she sped past Ava.

"I'll see you when you get there."

Ava laughed. "Don't count your chickens."

"You never beat me." Bailey bragged.

"There's a first time for everything." She shot back.

"Your determination is sexy."

Ava melted a little. "Stop trying to distract me."

Bailey exited, turned at the light and looked for Ava in her rearview mirror. She should have been behind her by now. "You alright back there, Beautiful?"

"Yep, I found a different way." She giggled.

"A different way?" Bailey checked behind her again. "You didn't mention a different way."

"Now why would I mention it?"

She pulled into the apartments in time to see Ava hop from her car and skip toward her apartment. "That's some shortcut."

"I'll leave the door unlocked." She replied. "Better hurry."

Bailey parked beside Ava. She took the stairs two at a time and pushed the door open to find a trail of clothes leading into the bedroom. Hearing a rush of water in the shower, she shed her clothes. Bailey found Ava hurriedly wrapping her hair in a satin scarf. She ducked from her reach and stepped under the water. Ava gave Bailey a sidelong glance, her lips parted and inviting. Eyes beckoning, the water cascaded down her shoulders and full breasts. Bailey moved behind Ava until their naked skin barely touched. She felt Ava's breath quicken and her eyes flickered to her lips. Bailey pulled her close and kissed her forehead. She kissed one cheek and then the other. Impatiently, Ava grabbed her face and kissed her. Bailey chuckled and nibbled on her bottom lip. After a moment, Ava loosened the grip and draped her arms around Bailey's shoulders. Skin to skin, a waterfall formed and splashed around their feet.

Bailey spun Ava around until she connected with the cold tile, reached down for her thighs and wrapped them around her waist. Talented fingers didn't waste time and cruised inside excited pussy. They moaned in unison and Ava found her lips again, already rotating her hips. Then Bailey found a spot, jolting Ava. Her breath left in a whoosh of air and for a moment she could do nothing but cling to her shoulders. Bailey rotated her fingers to another position and returned to it a few seconds later.

"Fuck." Ava whispered. She knew she was close and it was amazing Bailey brought her to the edge so quickly.

"Damn, you feel good." Bailey's voice came out a small growl.

"I do?"

"You do. Especially right here." Those musician's fingers twisted again and found the one spot – that one spot she knew made Ava lose her composed front.

"Shit!" Ava tried to backup. Quickly reminded of the tiled wall behind her, she succumbed to the sensation building in her loins. "Fuck me!"

Bailey obliged and met each enthusiastic thrust with renewed ardor, her fingers always coming back to that one spot. The moans bounced around the shower until one caught in Ava's throat. Her body shuddered and her gaze connected with Bailey's. She bit back words dangerously dangling from the tip of her tongue and closed her eyes in case Bailey could see the truth.

"Ava?" Bailey nuzzled her neck.

"Hmm?"

"The water is cold."

Ava giggled. "I hadn't noticed."

Bailey stepped out of the shower and set Ava on her feet. After turning off the water, she dried off and followed Ava into the bedroom. "I think I worked up an appetite."

"I'm absolutely famished! How about Chinese?"

"That'll work."

Ava pulled on a t-shirt and boy shorts. "I can't believe we ran into Daniel tonight."

"That motherfucker. I should have bashed his head in." Bailey picked up her boxers and jeans off the floor. She looked around for her shirt.

"Now what good would that have done?"

"It would have made me feel better."

Ava shook her head. "We did the best thing by denying it."

"He didn't believe us, Ava." Bailey zipped her pants.

"It's still our word against his though." Ava dialed the Chinese restaurant. "Do you want your usual?"

She nodded and waited for her to place the order. Something she couldn't name felt uneasy about lying. It was inevitable that Daniel would tell Cole. "I think we should tell Boss Lady."

"We can't do that."

"Think about it. If Daniel tells her first, she'll think we snuck around..."

"Which we have."

Bailey continued. "But if we tell her first and tell her the truth – that it just happened, she'll take it a whole lot better. You haven't been around her as much as I have, Baby. She hates being lied to."

"Everyone does, however, you were specifically told by Cole not to pursue me. One of us will probably lose their job to prevent drama and it won't be you." Ava laid it all out.

"There are other couples at Maxi's."

"We're not a couple."

Bailey fell silent. Taking a deep breath, she asked, "What if we were a couple?"

Ava's eyes grew big as her heart slammed against her rib cage. "W-What do you mean?"

"You know what I mean. Let's make it official."

"Are you serious?"

"Why wouldn't I be?" Bailey shrugged.

"You've never mentioned it before." Ava couldn't help but be a bit cautious.

"Doesn't mean I haven't thought about it."

"You didn't think I needed to be included in those thoughts you were having with yourself?"

Bailey sighed. "Are you really going to send me through a girly moment?"

"You're talking about a relationship, not fucking around. I'm sure I deserve a reason."

She swallowed the lump that mysteriously appeared in her throat. This wasn't the scene she envisioned all the times she rehearsed this moment. Questions weren't in any of those daydreams. "A reason?"

Ava's elation was quickly dissipating. "Do you have at least one reason? Have you really thought about what you're asking me?"

A pained expression passed over Bailey's features. She would just have to wing it. "Look, I'm not good at this okay. For the past few years, I've played around and ran from all types of commitment unless it was my music. I've never been good at monogamy so I stayed single. When you first started at the restaurant, my intention was to get in those panties and that was all. But..."

"But?"

"You make me crazy."

Ava blinked. "Excuse me?"

"You do. I'm crazy about how we talk, the chemistry we have. We have great conversation and our sex is hot." Bailey grinned and rushed on since she was on a roll. "You're supportive of my music and you're driven for your own goals. Your independence is sexy. Why not see where it goes?"

Ava felt the elation return while listening to her reasons, thinking how close Bailey's description was to her own daily musings. However, she needed a bit more. "Anything else?"

Bailey knew what she wanted to hear. For the first time in a long time, she meant the words she was about to say. "I care about you, Ava, enough to know that I don't want to see you with anyone else but me. I really don't know what or if that will evolve into anything more but I do know that I'm willing to try."

"I care about you too, Bailey. I want to keep things completely honest between us so I will admit that your past scares me. It makes me wonder what is so different about me than these other women who couldn't keep your attention." She shrugged.

Bailey reached for her hand, coaxing her into an embrace. "There is so much that is different about you. The biggest difference and the only one that really matters is how you make me feel. If you take a chance on me, you won't be disappointed."

Ava stared back into those beautiful, soft brown eyes and the last belt of her hesitation broke. She smiled. "How about we take a chance on each other?"

"Sounds fair." She smiled back before kissing Ava. Sudden pride engulfed her and she felt a weight lifted she hadn't wanted to acknowledge. Bailey traced a path of kisses down her neck. "Now we can tell Boss Lady."

"No Baby, we still can't."

Bailey pulled back. "Why not?"

"Besides that I haven't changed my mind about our jobs, there are so many busybodies at work I would prefer to keep them out of our business." Ava explained. "Please believe I want to shout this from the rooftops, but we can't go around making out at work anyway. The most important thing is that we know we're together."

Bailey knew that there was no use pressing the matter even before Ava finished. She let the dispute slide by and luxuriated in their new relationship status – even if it was a secret one. Mama always said to choose your battles. Bailey would give it a little time and bring it up later. Ava was bound to change her mind someday.

CHAPTER SIX

The morning announced its presence with thunderclaps and streaks of lightening. Loud booms woke Logan out of a sound sleep. It was so early it was still dark outside, she rolled over, buried her head under a pillow and tried to drift off again. The rain pelted the window mercilessly and after about twenty minutes of racket, she gave up and threw the covers off. Logan made a pot of coffee, scrambled some eggs and read an online newspaper. She went over a mental checklist of the day's errands and debated on whether to get an early start. The grocery store and other personal necessities were long overdue but the rain was certainly discouraging. Her ringing cell phone provided a distraction from the impending procrastination.

Logan didn't recognize the number. "Hello?"

"Hey Baby."

The voice, unmistakably familiar, pierced her heart. "How did you get this number?"

"We still have mutual friends." She teased. "Did you forget them when you sent out that mass text message? I was very hurt when I didn't get one too."

"You weren't meant to have it." Logan harshly replied. Bravery was much easier over the phone. "At the time I hadn't heard from you in months. It's been at least two months since I changed my number."

"Aww Baby. You know life is more hectic for me than you."

"Yeah, I know all about your hectic life."

"Don't you miss me even a little?" The voice pouted. "I've been aching to see you."

Logan was quiet and refused to admit the truth. Her scarred heart was far from healed. She didn't even know why she hadn't disconnected the call as soon as she heard her voice. Every time she pulled away, every time she thought she was free the cycle started up fresh and molten. "I don't want to see you."

"I'm at the door."

"How the fuck?" Logan looked out the peephole. There she was, slightly damp but just as beautiful. Her hands itched. "You need to fucking leave and forget where I live. I don't want to see you!"

"What did I do to you?" She placed one hand on the door. "Baby, I never wanted to hurt you. Please let me explain."

Logan cursed her fake bravado. She knew what would happen if she let her walk through that door. She knew she would give in. She fought against it for a few more seconds before unlocking the door. Her hair was shorter, a bob style that flattered her oval face. Her conservative attire of Capri pants and simple blouse was a front to the wantonness that existed. She stepped over the threshold, caressing Logan across the arm as she passed.

"Did you work last night?" She asked, depositing her purse on the table.

"No." Logan inhaled the soft, rosy scent infusing the air. Ever since high school, she'd worn the same flowery perfume. The smell would linger in the apartment for days.

"How've you been?"

"Just peachy." The sarcasm was evident but all she did was smile.

"Always so dramatic." She moved toward Logan, arms outstretched. "Aren't you going to forgive me?"

"You said you had an explanation." Logan moved around her and escaped toward the living room to take some deep breaths.

"Um, you already know my explanation. It's the same one I have every time."

"I can't deal with that anymore."

"And I can't deal with life without you." She cornered Logan by the couch. "I'm a wretch without you. I do nothing but think about you, fantasize about you...You don't know what it's like."

Logan snorted derisively. "I think I have a clue."

"I'll make more time. I promise."

"You said that last time."

"I've meant it every time." She succeeded in getting close enough to Logan to wrap her arms around her. "Let me try again."

Logan realized she wasn't holding on to her resolve as hard as she should be. Those practiced words were piercing her armor of denial and even though she felt every bit the hypocrite, she couldn't resist the mystique surrounding this woman. Logan grabbed her, roughly crushing their bodies together. She kissed Logan feverishly and began pulling at clothes as though they were suffocating her body. The disrobing didn't take long and Logan pushed her against the wall, one hand around her neck and the other reaching between her legs, mercilessly shoving two fingers in to saturated pussy.

"Mmm shit." Instinctively, she humped against the hard thrusts until Logan suddenly stopped.

"Did I tell you to ride my fingers?" Logan demanded.

She trembled. "No Daddi."

Logan twisted her fingers, enjoying the nail pricks on her shoulders. "You know what's going to happen now, right?"

"I'm sorry, Daddi."

"I don't want to hear it."

A smile played at the corners of her lips, so Logan pushed deeper and was rewarded with a low, guttural moan. Logan played with her a little longer before abruptly removing her fingers and pushed her toward the bed. She scampered away and stretched out on top of the comforter. Logan followed at a leisurely pace but walked into the bathroom instead. Before closing the door, she turned back to issue a warning.

"Don't fucking move."

"Yes, Daddi."

Logan sighed heavily and reached under the sink for the small, green duffel bag. While adjusting the buckles, she caught the mirror reflection and quickly looked away. Logan grabbed the lube but knew she wouldn't need much, she was always ready. Logan opened the door and caught her gently stroking her clit. Her heavy-lidded eyes beckoned with unrestrained lust. The dominant and the submissive was a game often played. Logan longed to make love to her – to share a connection. She dished out sexually-charged discipline instead. Logan stroked the dildo strapped to her hips.

"Did I tell you to start without me?"

"I was just so hot for you, Daddi, I couldn't wait."

"So do you want your fingers or do you want me?"

"I want you to fuck me."

A searing pain shot through Logan's heart, she ignored it and carried on with the make-believe. "You need to get the fuck over here and show me."

She rushed to the edge of the bed, quickly skimming her hands across Logan's small breasts. Logan acted as though her touch had no effect, even when she found that sensitive spot on her neck. The disinterested pretense eventually built up a tidal wave of lust and she finally resorted to begging. Her impatience hampered her willpower and within minutes she assumed a tamed position. On her hands and knees, pussy glistening with invitation, she pleaded with Logan to end her misery.

"Please Daddi. I need it."

Logan slipped a condom on and eyed her wiggling ass. She stepped forward and smacked her ample cheek with a resounding pop. She cried out from the sharp pleasure and backed into Logan, the dildo resting against her clit. Grinding against it, she whimpered Logan's name and locked her ankles around behind her thighs. Logan reached for the lube.

"Damn, please…fuck me!"

Their relationship thrived on raw, animalistic fucking. Logan entered her fiercely, spurred by hurt and frustration. Her reaction was always the same – pure exhilaration. The harder Logan pumped the wilder she became, clawing at the comforter as she screamed encouragement and direction. Logan shifted her to another position. She took each forceful thrust with ease.

"That's it! Tear it up Daddi!"

Logan gave her what she wanted and increased her tempo, figuring one more position should do it. She twisted her into a missionary and a scream of satisfaction mingled with the slurpy sounds of the determined dildo. Holding her hands, she rammed harder and faster, lost in the action of punishing her enflamed pussy. Logan felt tremors bubble up within her own heated sex but she kept pumping. The reality of the moment drifted into the corner of the room. Euphoric tingles spread through Logan, a besotted sensitivity to the slightest touch and the detonation followed soon after.

She heard her cry out – felt the strength pushing against her hands. Logan relaxed on top of her, drawing deep gulps of air and waited for her heartbeat to slow down. She rolled away, hearing the pop of the dildo leaving its home. Logan wasn't sure when she drifted off but she awoke startled, arms and legs spread across the bed. Logan sat up and looked around but knew she was already gone. The caramel phallus, still strapped to her body, mocked her. She painstakingly cleaned it and returned the toy to the green duffel bag. Logan took a shower and crawled back into bed. She ignored the feeling of self-loathing creeping around her psyche. If it wasn't for that rosy scent, Logan would've sworn she hadn't been there at all. That smell would linger in her apartment for days.

Rumors Ring True

Episode Three:
The Lies We Tell

CHAPTER ONE

The streets of downtown Dallas were busy every time of the day. Cars, driven by irritated humans, kissed each other's bumpers most of the morning. There were no smiles or joyfulness and the angry faces mixed with sleep peppered the faces of the workforce. Cole dodged the commuter death trap with a shortcut and came up behind Maxi's Place. She counted the vehicles scattered across the parking lot, proud of her diligent employees. Tuesday mornings were reserved for special cleanup duties. No one was exempt from attendance as even the smallest chore demanded attention. Whistling, she stomped through the back door and nodded at a few of the kitchen staff.

She unlocked her office and immediately fired up the computer to check her emails. Cole answered a few and deemed the rest unimportant enough to wait until later. She printed out a task list and headed toward the bar in search of Logan. The main dining area bustled with silverware polishing and vacuum cleaners. A group of three servers oiled the wooden trim around the room while another threesome dusted all the decorations. She didn't notice the succession of stares and whispers as she continued to the bar. Logan was nowhere to be seen.

"Ava, is Logan here?"

Ava stood up from behind the host stand. "I haven't seen her, Boss Lady."

Cole frowned. "Send her to me when she gets here."

"I'll tell her."

She turned and noticed a woman tapping on the front door. Unruly, golden curls were pulled back into a bun at the back of her head. Tan linen pants hugged her hips, showcasing curves with luscious hills and valleys. The pastel green blouse ruffled with a gust of wind exposing healthy, chocolate mounds. Her soft brown eyes held an unfathomable question.

Cole flashed her brightest smile before unlocking the door. "May I help you ma'am?"

"Yes, I need to confirm a reservation." She flicked her eyes over Cole. "I wasn't aware you were closed on Tuesday."

Cole stood back to let her in. "We conduct a deep clean on days we don't have prior appointments. What day is your reservation?"

"Saturday evening at eight."

"Under what name?"

"Kelsey Hopkins."

"I see it right here. Kelsey Hopkins. Bachelorette party." Cole handed the book back to Ava. "Congratulations on your nuptials."

Kelsey laughed. "Oh, I'm not the bride. I'm the maid of honor. I have to make sure she has an awesome time."

"I'll make sure it's a night she never forgets."

"You look like you're good at that."

"I could be." Cole moved toward the door. "Have you been here before?"

"Yes. Many, many times."

"Too bad we haven't met before."

"We'll have to find a way to make up for lost time then."

Cole watched that delectable backside swish away before locking the door. She made a quick weekend plan and returned to the bar.

"Boss Lady!" Ava called out. "Line three."

"Always something." She grabbed the bar extension. "Cole Washington."

"This is the manager of the club?" The small, female voice had a deep Southern drawl.

"This is the owner. How may I help you?"

"Hold on, my mama wants to talk to you."

Her mama? Cole impatiently listened to the shuffle.

"Is this the manager?" An older version with the same twang demanded.

"This is the owner."

"Daisy, I thought you said this was the manager!"

"Ma'am, I am the manager as well."

"Well, why didn't you just say so?"

Cole sighed. "Ma'am, how may I help you?"

"No need for hostility. I am looking for my son, Danny."

"Danny?" Cole glanced at the host stand. "Your son?"

"Yes, ever since he moved up to the city, I barely get to talk to him and now that his number's disconnected..."

"Um, ma'am..." Cole tried to interrupt.

"I just don't know any other way to get in touch with him. I'd have thought he'd call by now. I guess he don't worry too much about me like I do about him."

"I understand. I will give him the message."

"I do appreciate it. Let me give you my number."

"Wouldn't he have your number ma'am?"

"I haven't talked to him in so long, he might've forgotten it."

Cole grinned and scribbled the number on a bar napkin. After assuring Daniel's mother once more, she hung up. "Ava, where's Daniel?"

Ava avoided Cole's eyes. "He hasn't gotten here yet."

"It's amazing how many of my employees don't think that punctuality is a necessity." She stalked toward the kitchen, finding Tasha inspecting sauté pans.

"So that's what everyone is talking about." Tasha smirked at her.

"What is everyone talking about now?" At times, the constant chatter annoyed Cole.

"Your outfit. I don't think I've ever seen you in jeans before." Tasha replied. "Long night?"

"Actually, yes it was."

"Who was it this time?"

Cole frowned. "Excuse me?"

"You know what, I don't want to know." She suddenly fumed. "I don't want to know which filly in your stable had you up all night."

"Filly in my stable?" Cole leaned in close. "For your information, I was at my mother's house painting her guest room."

She enjoyed the shock sweep across Tasha's features. Words escaped her sharp tongue and she could do nothing but stare. "I…"

"Exactly. I'm sorry I disappointed your assumption of me."

Tasha's anger returned. "Don't get all pious with me, Cole. I'll admit I assumed you were with a woman last night but it isn't like that isn't your usual habit."

"What does it matter what I do?" Cole shot back. "Last time I checked, I'm a grown ass Stud."

She took a step back. "You know, you're absolutely right. I have no idea why it matters to me that you're devoid of any type of commitment. I'm not the one afraid to sleep alone."

Cole watched Tasha stomp off to another part of the kitchen before she walked back to the office. What the fuck did it matter where she was last night? She slammed the door and shuffled some papers around. One truth about Tasha was her ability to jump to conclusions. It was one of their constant arguments that Cole never won. Tasha needed to worry about her own household and the lackluster relationship she cherished so much. Plus, she wasn't afraid to sleep alone. Cole didn't like sleeping alone. There's a difference. She went from normal to crazy in a matter of seconds for no reason and Cole wasn't chasing after the madness. In the past, she would cater to Tasha's mood and attempt to fix the issue. Cole refused to play the game this time.

CHAPTER TWO

L ogan heard the front door close with a soft click. She sat up, swung her legs over the side of the bed and peered down at the leather apparatus still strapped to her hips. She stood and released the buckles, letting the harness fall around her ankles. Bending over to pick it up, Logan glanced at the clock.

"Shit." She brushed her teeth in the shower and ten minutes later, she was barreling down the freeway toward Maxi's Place.

The padding of her helmet muted the outside traffic and Logan's self-loathing flared back up. She felt powerless against her traitorous emotions and the resulting decisions. Logan never believed her excuses for giving in to the weakness again. She rationalized it was fate that brought them together. Love united them. Hate kept them apart. A cool morning jog ended up hot and steamy in the girls' locker room. The encounter erupted into frequent liaisons wherever and whenever they could. Logan didn't usually fuck around with straight girls but Allie was irresistible with a tinge of danger and fascination.

Absolutely besotted after that day, Logan made concessions she never thought she would, including dealing with a jealous boyfriend was at the top of that list. They snuck around for a few months, before the meathead caught on. Dread and worry overtook her as Allie explained what her boyfriend wanted in return for his silence. As much as she loved Allie, Logan couldn't commit to the conditions. He was Allie's boyfriend. How did a threesome become the solution? Logan urged her to forget about him, hoping their love would propel them toward a future. She learned you don't always get what you hope for. Devastation didn't accurately describe what Logan felt when she chose him instead. Senior year continued in a depressing blur but she didn't give up hope that the girl of her dreams would come to her senses. But it never happened. Allie ignored her pleading looks and with absolute finality. Before she ceased all communication, she reminded Logan of what could've kept them together and refused to understand any other side of the situation. To Allie, sex didn't always include your heart and it didn't matter what gender. She was pregnant and married shortly after graduation.

Logan accepted defeat, vowed never again and went on with her life. She attended college on a track scholarship, enjoyed the feminine attention and felt liberated. However, Allie popped up in her dreams. Logan would awaken, drenched in sweat and bombarded with memories. She'd shake it off and find a pretty woman to kiss on. Then senior year, she was invited to a wedding of one of her fellow students. The ceremony seemed endless and the reception was barely underway before Logan contemplated a good time to duck out. She perused the room for the happy couple and her eyes fell upon a familiar sight.

Her heart slammed against her chest in disbelief but that flawless profile was unmistakable. Allie stood with a bridesmaid, loosely holding a glass of champagne. Logan couldn't help but appreciate the wonderful affects motherhood had on her hips and ass. Allie turned and met her gaze, leaving her frozen and oddly vulnerable. Logan watched the recognition play across her features. They met in the middle and exchanged an awkward hug.

"How cliché is this?" Allie smiled.

"Yes, it certainly is a small world." She replied.

"I didn't know you knew the bride."

"I don't. I know the groom."

"I guess so. You look good."

"Thanks, so do you."

She rolled her eyes. "What you mean to say is that I look different."

"I'm sure we both look different." Logan compromised.

"No," She scanned her from head to toe. "You definitely look good."

"Thank you."

"Why don't we find a quiet place to talk."

Logan hesitated, remembering she was on her way out the door. She weighed the consequence and decided a little conversation never hurt anyone. They settled at an empty table in the corner away from the reveling crowd. Another awkward second passed and they shared a nervous laugh.

"So much has changed in just a few years." Allie piped up.

"I bet. How old is your kid now?"

"Which one?"

"You have more than one now?"

"Well, that's one of two things meathead is good at." She wryly answered. "I have two boys."

"That's a handful."

"You have no idea. He doesn't help me with the little heathens at all. Don't get me wrong," Allie hastily added. "I love my children but our Mamas didn't lie when they talked about us."

Logan nodded. "Of course."

"Truth is, I'm bored. I haven't had a job since before the second one was born and only so he could finish school. He comes home wanting sex and doesn't care I've dealt with his children all day."

"I thought your life would turn out differently."

She smirked. "Did you really?"

Logan shrugged. "You never know."

"Well, it could be worse." She replied. "At least I don't want for anything. I live in a beautiful home. Drive a great car. What more could you ask for?"

Logan thought of quite a few things but didn't share her suggestions. Something about her situation sent up warning flags and she suddenly had the urge to leave.

She waved her hand, swatting away the awkwardness. "Enough about me. What about you? Dating anyone?"

Logan blushed. "Here and there."

"Here and there? Translation, you're a player."

"I wouldn't say that. If you must know, I'm busy with school most of the time. Relationships aren't really high on my list right now."

She sighed. "If you're smart, you'll keep it that way."

They continued to meet for lunch every few weeks and only focused on the present. Sexual tension was nonexistent and Logan felt a genuine friendship develop between them. She asked about who Logan was dating and offered advice. Logan listened to the daily saga she dealt with at home. In hindsight, all the clues were there but ignorance was bliss.

One hot afternoon, they met at a popular Italian restaurant and sipped wine in the cabana on the terrace. The wind blew warm air against the thick curtains causing a hard flap against the table. Every so often the force pushed the curtain higher, knocking over the salt and pepper grinder. The serene moment took on an illusion of a Mediterranean villa. The wine relaxed their tongues and soon the flapping curtains blended into the white noise of the afternoon. Logan sunk down into the cushioned wicker chair, closed her eyes against the breeze and let the stress of classes ebb from her shoulders.

"You know," Allie broke the silence. "No, nevermind."

Logan opened her eyes. "What?"

"Nothing."

"Just say it."

"Have you ever wondered about us?"

Logan stopped mid-sip. Her stomach tightened as she searched for a response? "About us?"

"So you're playing stupid now?" She teased. "Or is this convenient forgetfulness?"

"Well..." Logan croaked. "I mean, of course I have. We had some steamy months together."

"Months?"

"Yeah, months." The bitterness welled up in Logan's throat. "Then, as we know, stuff happened."

She had the temerity to avoid her intense eyes. "That was painful for both of us."

Logan didn't respond. Painful was an understatement. The devastation obsessed Logan for months. Graduation was a blur of maroon caps and halter top pictures. She spent the summer in isolation trying to repair her emotional well-being. This conversation muddled her intoxicated senses and she searched for an excuse.

"Well, that's all in the past now."

"It doesn't have to be."

It doesn't have to be. Logan braked at a traffic light and returned to the present. A defining moment she couldn't change. A regrettable decision no matter how you spun it. She parked and walked around to the patio doors by the bar. She scanned for Cole before quickly slipping behind the bar.

~~~~~

"You're always working hard." Tre dropped a cardboard box on the floor next to the host stand.

Ava nodded. "Boss Lady likes hard workers."

"I see that." Tre watched for a moment, admiring the surreal glow around her face. "I really appreciate you helping me get this job, Ava."

"I didn't get you the job, Tre." Ava replied. "I only referred you."

She grinned. "If you say so. Every Lesbian on campus wants to work at Maxi's. I've applied here at least three times. The fourth time, I put you down as a reference and boom, I have a job. My luckiest day was taking that web design class."

Ava shook her head. "Like I said, I did nothing but provide a reference. Just don't make me look bad."

"I wouldn't dream of it."

"Ava, you up there?" Cole's voiced boomed over the intercom.

Ava jumped. "Yes, Boss Lady."

"Has Logan or Daniel showed up yet?"

"Logan is here."

"Send her to my office."

"Yes ma'am." She watched Logan walk the green mile with a pang of empathy for the ordeal waiting in the office.

Cole answered the timid knock with a curt command. "Come in, Logan."

The door opened slowly, revealing an unusually disheveled Logan. Her hair had grown out some and darkness creeped around her eyes. An old, faded t-shirt and jeans hung off her slender frame. She shoved her hands in her pockets and avoided Cole's gaze.

Cole's chair creaked as she sat back. "You are my lead bartender and besides from training staff, I pay you extra to be an example for other employees. For the past month, you have been consistently late. This isn't like you."

"I know, Boss Lady." Logan mumbled.

"I'm assuming you have an excuse."

She hesitated. "I'm not sleeping at night. When I do, I oversleep."

Cole studied her face. "You worried about something?"

"No."

"How long have you had these sleepless nights?"

"The last two months."

"Have you seen a doctor?"

"I haven't had the time."

"Make the time. What's the point in having insurance if y'all don't use it?" Cole sighed. "See a doctor and buy a loud alarm clock. Get back to work."

"Yes, Boss Lady." Logan almost ran over an incoming Tasha as she made a hasty exit.

Tasha watched her retreat. "I see you've been scaring the employees again."

"No more than usual." Cole stiffly replied. She eyed the covered tray Tasha set on her desk. "What's that?"

"A peace offering."

"A peace offering?"

"Yep." Tasha removed the napkin, revealing Cole's coveted sandwich and fresh potato chips.

"Are those chips the new recipe you came up with?" She stood to wash her hands.

"Yes, they are."

Cole savored the first bite. "Thank you, but why is this a peace offering?"

Tasha grimaced. "I was out of line earlier. I had no right to say that to you."

"I accept your apology."

"I didn't say it was…oh, nevermind." She stole a chip from the plate. "How's Margie?"

"Feisty and ornery." Cole replied. "She still likes to supervise."

Tasha smiled. "She is very good at supervising."

"Remember when we planted her vegetable garden?"

"Oh my goodness. Margie was very regal sitting in that comfy lounge chair, sipping lemonade. We didn't do anything right that day."

"She misses you."

Tasha averted her eyes. "I'll give her a call."

"She'd like that." Cole felt the shift in the atmosphere and resentment bubbled up. "How's Kai?"

She stiffened. "Kai is fine. Strange of you to ask."

"Why is it strange?"

"Because you don't particularly…care for her."

Cole shrugged. "We're friends, right? I worry about you."

Tasha rolled her eyes. "What are you worried about?"

"Are you happy?"

"This is out of the blue." She stalled. That was a tough question to answer.

"I was wondering."

"That's a nasty habit."

"You just don't seem happy."

"I'm fine. Kai is fine." Tasha didn't hide her irritation. "We're both fine."

"Where is she working now?"

Her sharp intake of breath warned Cole. She knew their truce was about to evaporate but her resistance was weak. Cole wanted to show Tasha a little about her perfect relationship. Kai butterflied her way through a dependent existence while Tasha footed the bill.

"Do you have a point to your question?" Tasha finally asked.

"I'm curious."

"Why?"

"Why not? It's an honest question." She shrugged. "Kai changes jobs a lot."

"And she's home every night." Tasha retorted. "Something you never were. You should know that money comes and goes, Cole."

"Not if you know how to make it multiply."

A tiny shiver erupted within Tasha at the cocky tone. She cursed her body's weakness and stood. "I don't know why I even tried."

Remorse dampened Cole's victory. "Look Tasha, I didn't mean…"

"Forget it Cole. Enjoy your sandwich."

Daniel jumped out of the way as Tasha barreled past. "Morning, Miss Tasha."

"Daniel, get in here and close the door!" Cole bellowed.

He jumped at her tone and attempted a smile. "Morning, Boss Lady."

Cole checked her watch. "Don't you mean afternoon. I may be older but I can still tell time. However, even with your obvious youth, you can't tell time. I really don't want to think that I employ people who can't tell time. So please, reassure me that you can tell time."

"I…I can tell time."

"Good." Cole smiled. "Then why are you late and more importantly, why didn't you call and tell me you would be late?"

"Well, I overslept."

"You overslept?"

"Yes, I overslept."

"Seems to be an epidemic." She sighed and rubbed her temples. "Did you set an alarm?"

"On my cell phone."

"The same cell phone that you didn't use to call and tell me you'd be late?"

For once, Daniel was mute. Cole saw the uncertainty flicker over his features and realized her frustration wasn't helping. "Why did you oversleep, Daniel?"

"I'm sorry, Boss Lady. It won't happen again."

Suddenly tired, Cole allowed him to ignore her question. "Make sure it doesn't."

"Yes, ma'am."

"And call your mother."

"Ma'am?"

"I had the pleasure of speaking with your mother this morning. Apparently, she doesn't have your new number."

Daniel was surprised but quickly recovered. "I gave Mama the number. She must have misplaced it."

"Make sure she gets it."

"Yes ma'am."

Cole stared at the door a long time waiting for Tasha to reappear. She'd heard that speech a few times but it was something about the tone of her voice that pierced the built-up bravado. Her words, albeit truthful, stung Cole's pride. She had a business to run and late nights were a part of the responsibilities. Cole shouldn't have cared what Tasha thought about her actions and until lately, usually didn't. If only their relationship hadn't experienced so many rough patches, maybe…Cole stopped the travel down memory lane. There was shit to do.

CHAPTER THREE

The perks of being a musician were practically endless but the best was exemption from cleaning the restaurant. Bailey started out waiting tables at Maxi's Place. Ambition waited in the wings while she smiled and bowed for tips. Occasionally, Bailey accompanied her quartet of older siblings to appease her musical fix. She didn't think she'd ever get a break and then fate intervened. A brilliant idea occurred to Cole to host a talent show for local artists. The winner became a headliner at the restaurant. It took some smooth talking but Bailey convinced her brothers and sisters to enter. Winning shocked everyone except Bailey, whose confidence was so high she launched an aggressive marketing campaign. They recorded tracks and sold singles after every show. The fans poured out of the woodwork, eager to lend support to a Dallas native.

She strolled in through the stage door and nodded at her sister, setting up her drums. "Sup."

"Is the world ending?" Sheila asked.

"What are you talking about?" Bailey laid her case on the piano.

"You're early. Alvin will be mad you beat him."

"Alvin needs a life."

"Don't we all."

Bailey glanced toward the host stand. As predictable as federal taxes, Ava stood at her station. Her heart skipped and a smile creased her features but frowned when Tre appeared next to Ava. Suspicion clouded Bailey's eyesight since that Stud arrived at Maxi's. She was too close all the time.

"Are you here to practice, Bailey?" Alvin announced his presence, huffing and puffing with his double bass.

She shot him a dirty look. "No Alvin, I'm here to haunt the place."

"We can arrange that." He retorted.

"You know what, Alvin? You can…"

Sheila intervened. "Ok, you two. That's not going to solve anything. Alvin, leave Bailey alone. At least she was on time."

Alvin grumbled something about being spoiled and sulked while tuning his instrument. Bailey reluctantly returned to her responsibilities, however, she couldn't concentrate and missed a few cues. She caught Ava looking toward the stage. Reassured by her smile, Bailey puffed up a bit at the silent invitation. With Ava as an audience, she added a bit more flair than usual on a solo and received some questioning looks. Reluctantly, Bailey focused on rehearsal.

Later she waited in the back parking lot for Ava to come out. Practice melted away self-imposed stress and she was ready for a little feminine attention. Her exuberance screeched to a halt when Tre stepped out behind Ava. Her fist tightened when Ava laughed at something Tre said, stopping to hold her stomach. She noticed Bailey's car and waved Tre off.

Ava leaned into the window. "Hey sexy."

Bailey grinned. "Hey."

"Your sound was great today." She smiled back. "Were you showing out for me?"

"What makes you think that?"

"You seemed so enthusiastic."

She licked her lips. "I'm always enthusiastic about things I put my mouth on."

Ava blushed. "What am I going to do with you?"

"Invite me back to your place and I'll give you a list."

"Aww Baby, I have a study group but I'll call you afterwards." Ava's heart flipped at her crestfallen face. "You know I'd rather spend my spare time with you but this semester is kicking my ass."

"No, I understand. I didn't mean to guilt you."

"I promise I'll make it up to you." She looked around the parking lot before leaning closer for a kiss.

Bailey grabbed her shirt, pulling Ava closer. She slipped her tongue between her fleshy lips. Ava dueled with her for a few seconds before pushing back.

"Damn, I'd rather invite you over." It didn't take much for Bailey to weaken her knees.

She chuckled. "Go to your study group and call me later."

"Promise you, I will." Ava stole another peck and jogged the short distance to her car.

Bailey watched the small sedan leave before she turned her car toward home. Ava's hard semester meant more studying, less attention. An alien concept for Bailey to understand and she wasn't prepared for it. She understood the hard work and dedication needed to keep up a grade point average. The back burner wasn't territory her ego understood.

She tossed the car keys on the coffee table, turned on the TV and went to the kitchen. After warming up Ava's leftover meatloaf, Bailey settled down on the couch. Addicted to the true crime channels, her eyes soaked up all the bloody reality they could. A special on grandmother's who murdered ended and Bailey checked the time. She contemplated texting her. Ava promised she'd call later. It was definitely later.

Bailey tried not to stalk the clock and sat down at the computer. She cued up a track, going through the motions of perfecting the sound, a funky Cuban jazz feel Bailey loved so much. Ava loved this track and voiced her criticism over a few changes Bailey made. However, it seemed Tre also enjoyed Ava's criticism in her quest to become the perfect employee. These days Tre saw more of Ava then Bailey did. Ava insisted on their relationship remaining secret for the sake of their jobs. Unbridled jealousy amplified every time competition appeared at Maxi's Place. Realizing she had a possessive nature plagued her for days. A simple embrace caused a ricochet of emotion. A sensation of coming home cloaked her unprepared soul and the tears welled. Bailey needed Ava. A four letter word bounced off the sides of her gray matter. A four letter word she didn't recall ever feeling before - all because of her. Absolute joy came over Bailey from the thought of Ava's existence and she wouldn't allow anyone to take away someone so precious.

She jumped at her ringing her phone. "Hello?"

"Hey Baby." Ava cooed. "I just looked at my watch. What are you doing?"

"Working on some tracks." Bailey replied.

"Mmm. If I was there, I'd put you to work."

"I'd definitely work it out."

"How do you do that?" Her voice dipped.

"Do what?"

"Make me wet over the phone?"

"Hey Ava, what did you get for number 8?" Tre was so close to Ava, Bailey could hear her breathing.

"Be there in a minute. I'm on the phone." Ava responded. "I called to tell you I would be another hour or so. Will you be up?"

"I'll wait up."

"Mmm. I'll call you when I'm on my way."

"Okay." Bailey sighed. She'd have to keep an eye on Tre and her pursuit of an education.

~~~~~

Cole did something completely out of her comfort zone and a guarantee her evening was a solitary one. She went home. Another good tip taught by Aunt Maxi was to treat her home as a sanctuary. A woman hadn't stepped foot in Cole's house in a long time. Not since Tasha. She pulled into the townhome garage and climbed the stairs to the second level. She flicked on the living room lights and glanced over her modern angular furniture, which was high on taste but low on comfort. Cole flipped through the preset station on the radio to drown out the silence. After hearing the same song on three different channels, she popped in her own CD. Sipping from a highball of brown liquor, she rummaged the kitchen for a snack but was greeted with bare cupboards instead. She ordered a pizza. Cooking wasn't a strong suit and another reason Tasha attracted her. Tasha hated anything that wasn't homemade.

"Food is love, Baby and some kid making eight dollars an hour is not taking the care and patience needed to create magnificent food."

Tasha proceeded to design a homemade pizza with such heavenly flavors, Cole bought a pizza oven and put it on the lunch menu. As she chewed the popular pizza chain, Cole gave Tasha her props once again. Mama always said Tasha would be the one that got away. Lately, Cole's life was a favorite subject around the restaurant. She didn't think her actions were all that scandalous, at least not enough for Tasha to have a tantrum about it. They weren't together anyway. Cole finished off the drink and checked all the locks. Slipping into bed, she remembered why she didn't like to sleep at home.

The single life possessed a multitude of benefits, although sleeping in an empty bed wasn't one. True, the entire bed was at her disposal and she spread her limbs in every direction, searching for a comfortable position. She always ended up on one side. Sleep was a hard fought achievement when she was at home. Anywhere else, Cole dropped off within minutes of her head hitting the pillow, except at the one place she should feel most comfortable.

CHAPTER FOUR

The rest of the week was business as usual. The people came. They ate great food, guzzled intoxicating beverages and listened to soulful music. All was well to the many satisfied customers and they would never feel the underlying tension floating through the restaurant. Nonetheless, the employees sensed a rift in their atmosphere and rumors circulated. Kitchen staff buzzed about the curt conversations laced with sarcastic professionalism between Cole and Tasha during menu reviews. The servers whispered to the host stand how they avoided each other in the dining room. The bartenders, ever the elusive click, discussed their own theories on what may have happened. Annoyed by the obvious chatter, Cole broke up gossip groups most of Friday dinner shift. She delivered a lecture about attention to work responsibilities before Saturday brunch. Tasha smirked as she strolled through the dining room.

Cole spent the afternoon in her office, brooding and shuffling paperwork. The fact that Tasha's words even bugged her was amazing. Cole lived her life by her own rules and a woman either accepted that or she didn't. It didn't matter to Cole what she decided.

There was always another woman somewhere. Tasha was the exception. She had a way of placing a mountain of guilt on Cole's shoulders much akin to her mother, Margie. Her stomach growled but Cole refused to go begging for a sandwich. A part of her knew this was no way to run a business. Stubborn pride makes fools out of the most intelligent of people.

She finally emerged around shift change and avoided the kitchen for as long as she could. She sauntered around the dining room for a spot inspection and stopped at the host stand to skim the wait list. She gave a couple of slacking bartenders a quick pep talk and checked the patio for any stray glassware. Finally, Cole pushed through the stainless steel, swinging door. Even with all the bustle, she spotted Tasha by the pastry line. Their eyes locked and for a brief second she caught a tenderness Cole thought no longer existed between them.

Tasha broke the stare and took a deep breath. She watched Cole approach and realized she held on to her anger as long as she could. She also knew she had no right to be angry. Tasha met her in the middle of the kitchen. A hush came over the kitchen and ears strained to hear a snippet of conversation.

Tasha spoke first. "Have you eaten?"

Relief flooded Cole's eyes. "No, I haven't."

"I'll make you a sandwich." She reached out and touched her arm before walking off.

Cole gathered her senses and glared around the kitchen to get the staff working again. Back in the office, she analyzed the switch in Tasha's mood. The action was completely unexpected but welcome nonetheless. Although, Tasha wasn't the type to give in first unless she felt she was truly wrong. On the other hand, Cole speculated it could be an elaborate plan for the defenses to drop and then Tasha would make her move of revenge. Cole tensed at the soft knock on the door.

"Come in."

"Here you go." Tasha waited until the first bite. "I don't want to fight with you, Cole. It's not productive for the restaurant and you're still a friend, no matter our past."

"I feel the same way, Sha Sha."

Her heart flipped. "Good. Enjoy your sandwich."

The news of the makeup circulated just as quickly as the fight. Cole went about her duties with a little pep in her step. The night crowd began to thicken and the waitstaff ran a relay from the kitchen to the bar. The bartenders served up smooth lines and dared patrons to loosen a few inhibitions. The night was full of exuberant and intoxicated faces, vying for a place at the bar. Cole noticed Kai standing at the bar, drinking and brightly colored in an orange polo shirt and tan jeans. At least twice a month, Kai found her way in for a handout from Tasha.

"How're you doing, Kai?"

"Big pimpin' Cole!" Kai shook her hand. "I'm one hundred, know what I'm sayin'?"

"Glad to hear it." She delivered a practiced smile. "How's the drink?"

Kai saluted with her highball. "Only the best at your establishment, Boss. I came to visit the little woman and add my groove to the social atmosphere. Ya dig?"

Cole nodded. "I dig. Well, have a good time."

"Appreciate it."

The cliché of opposites attracting was certainly the case when it came to Tasha and Kai. Cole refused to understand how an ambitious, driven woman could actually be in love with a lazy bum. The whole relationship was such a downgrade. Cole took a turn through the kitchen on the pretense of checking on ticket times. Tasha greeted her with a bright smile.

"How's it look out there."

"Nice and busy." Cole replied. "You have a visitor."

Tasha blinked but that was the only reaction she gave. The bright smile never faltered. "I didn't know she was coming in tonight. Please tell Logan to send me her tab."

She nodded. "Okay."

"This isn't a problem, is it?"

"No, of course not. I was just letting you know she was here." Cole smiled and walked away. She didn't want to burn any newly constructed bridges.

Tasha exhaled. *Why was she here?* The restaurant was her one true escape from Kai and every time she showed up for free booze and a meal, Tasha's personal space was violated. Kai stayed under the illusion that the practice of showing up at Maxi's Place was cute instead of a distraction. The last worry she needed on a Friday night was Kai's drunken behavior. She found Kai perched on a barstool, ordering another drink. Logan poured a double shot of the expensive cognac and moved on to the next customer. She finally noticed Tasha and exhibited an elaborate greeting.

"There's my woman." Kai grabbed Tasha and kissed her. "Damn, you're sexy in all that chef shit."

Tasha backed out of her arms. "Don't drink too much or you'll have to wait for me to take you home."

"Sonny is on her way." Kai took a sip and grinned. "She'll take me home."

She sighed at the thought of two freeloading motherfuckers to pay for. "Make sure you eat something, okay?"

"Aww, is the little woman worried about me?"

"No, I don't need you getting drunk. I do work here."

Cole watched Tasha return to the kitchen. There was nothing worse than wasting your life. She would forever ponder why they weren't together anymore and what it would take to get her back. Every time she had it figured out, Tasha reminded her how far off track she was. Cole was out of ideas on getting her attention.

"Boss Lady, the bachelorette party has arrived."

Cole took her time sauntering toward the host stand, stopping to shake a hand or two before making an appearance. "Ava, I have a guest?"

"Yes, Ms. Kelsey Hopkins." Ava nodded toward a group of giggling women. One of them was wearing a plastic, princess crown with a white mesh veil hanging from it.

It wasn't hard to pick out those bouncy curls and titillating curves filling out the short, black cocktail dress. Her style was still tasteful in comparison with her cohorts' ensembles of leggings and booty shorts. Kelsey smiled at Cole's approach and accepted her extended hand.

"Ms. Hopkins, how wonderful to see you again." Cole's smile dripped sugar. "The night can officially begin."

"I did come to have a good time." She batted her lashes. "Please call me Kelsey."

"Only if you call me Cole, Kelsey. I will make it my personal responsibility that you have a good time."

"Thank you, Cole." Kelsey remembered the woman in the veil. "Let me introduce you to the bride, Debra."

"Congratulations on your impending nuptials. Allow me to escort your party to the VIP section."

"VIP!" Debra exclaimed. "Kels, you went all out, girl!"

"Only the best for your last night of being single." Kelsey replied, taking Cole's arm and pressing her breasts against her.

Cole led the way through the thickening crowd. The VIP waitstaff were the best in the restaurant, usually trainers who earned the right to make good money. They snapped to attention and greeted the women as they sat down at the various round tables. Cole held a chair for Kelsey at the main table. She glanced down into voluptuous cleavage before meeting her eyes.

"If there is anything else I can do for you, Kelsey, don't hesitate to send one of your servers after me."

"Why, thank you. I'm sure you could handle any need I have, Cole."

~~~~~

Tasha took a break from the line to check on Kai at the bar. Sonny worried her more than her no-good girlfriend. Kai blindly followed her into every stupid action imaginable and it was a complete turn-off. She wasn't in the same spot and after a quick scan, Tasha knew Kai had left. She never wandered far from the bar. Here it was the busiest night of the week and she was worried about a grown woman. Only Kai would show up when there was an hour wait and no one could keep an eye on her. Walking back to the kitchen, Tasha paused at a few tables to ask about the taste of the food. The delighted looks on the faces of the patrons warmed her heart and reminded her of why she loved to cook. It was the only solace she had these days. Tasha peeped at the VIP section in time to see Cole schmooze the bachelorette party, seeming to pay particular attention to a busty beauty in a black dress. Tasha recognized the seductive smirk Cole was profiling and knew that the wolf was circling her prey. She returned to her haven of pots and pans, disappointment torturing her subconscious.

Tasha knew why she cared about Cole's activity. She also knew why she shouldn't Cole was an attractive, single stud and owed no one explanations. Since Cole was a creature of habit, Tasha jumped to the same conclusion with the rest of the staff. Her tailor made suits were imbedded into her swagger and Cole was rarely seen in anything else. Spending the night away from home was the only logical explanation for her to wear jeans to the restaurant. It was ironic how every good trait Kai possessed were no longer important to her.

CHAPTER FIVE

Despite Cole's attraction, Kelsey Hopkins was also a paying customer. The party package she paid for in advance warranted extra attention. Cole made several trips through VIP, making sure drinks were filled and everyone was having a good time. She felt the determined stare or provocative grin Kelsey flashed whenever she made an appearance. The bride was too bombed to notice and only concerned when the next cocktail would arrive. Kelsey took those as opportunities to flirt with Cole and drop more than a few hints.

"Cole, may I have a word with you?" Kelsey caught Cole at the stairs.

She felt the squeeze of fingers against her biceps. "Are you having a good time?"

"Yes, of course. I appreciated the shout out from the stage by the way."

"We aim to please. So what can I do for you?"

"Is there a place where we can hear each other better?"

Cole grabbed her elbow and walked to the office. She closed the door behind them, turned off her headset and waited. If she wanted to make the first move, Cole would let her. She needed to hurry up though. It was a busy night.

"This is a nice office." Kelsey said suddenly. "It smells like you."

"How do I smell?"

"Sexy."

Cole chuckled. "Thank you."

"My pleasure."

"So what did you want to talk to me about?"

"Honestly, I didn't think past being alone with you." Kelsey admitted.

"So what did you think would happen?"

"I was hoping you'd work that out for me."

"I can definitely work that out for you." Cole reached her within seconds, grabbing her around the waist and taking control of her lips.

Kelsey responded with a dreamy sound and thrust her tongue into Cole's mouth. She clutched at strong shoulders, her body tingling from the hands which held her so roughly. They flitted down to her ass. Cole pushed her toward the couch. Kelsey spun around and made Cole sit so she could straddle her lap. She pulled the dress straps down and thrust her breasts against Cole's face. Kelsey gasped when those lips were suddenly tender and grazed erect nipples.

"I saw you watching me all night." She cupped Cole's head. "You had such a determined stare. It made me think about what you would do to me."

Cole nuzzled her neck and moved a hand between Kelsey's legs, swiftly pushing aside the thin strip of fabric. "What did you think I would do?"

"Mmm, shit. I thought you would...um, wait. Is the door locked?" She frantically glanced at it like someone would walk in at any moment.

"Yes, it's locked." Cole stroked her clit.

"Y-You sure?"

Cole's fingers found the spot she was looking for and put an end to her worry. She slid into hot, soaking pussy. Velvet walls sucked her into an endless depth and instinctively began a deliberate rotation. Cole shifted her thumb back around to give her swollen clit a little more attention.

"Oh shit!" Kelsey pulled her head back to her breasts and humped harder against Cole's exploring fingers.

The knock on the door was loud and they jumped. "Hey Boss Lady, we need your expertise out here!"

"I'll be there in a minute!" Cole shouted, instantly irritated by the interruption.

"You don't think they heard me, do you?" She asked.

"No, I don't think they did." Cole removed her fingers, smiling at Kelsey's jerk reaction. "What are you doing later?"

"I am at a party going on out there." Kelsey smirked and stood from her lap with unsteady legs.

Cole pointed at the bathroom door. "You're welcome to use the facilities."

"How convenient." Kels smiled at her reflection in the mirror. Her lips were swollen from kisses and smeared with lipstick. She took a moment to straighten her dress, reapply her makeup and fix her hair as much as possible. To think she's spent two hours on her hair tonight for a few minutes of finger fucking. Cole appeared and she felt the grind against her ass.

"Mmm. Don't you need to go do something?"

"Yes, I do. Meet me later." Cole demanded, washing her hands.

"Ask me later."

"Why later?" She led her to the door.

"I need time for the alcohol to wear off." She strutted back to her table of friends. Wetness gushed against her pussy when she sat down and caught Debra staring at her. "What?"

"Where did you run off to?" Speech slurred, she pointed a manicured nail at Kelsey.

"To the little girl's room."

"That was a long time just to go to the bathroom."

It seemed like seconds. "Can't I have a little privacy?"

"Don't get huffy with me, bitch." Debra said. "I was just showing concern for your ass. I thought you were sick or something."

Thankfully, her tirade was cut short by the arrival of a tray of shots. The waiter called them Berry Bombers. Debra didn't care as she threw back two of them in quick succession leaving Kelsey to her thoughts. She needed a clear head so no more alcohol for the night. The popularity of Maxi's Place was legendary and the wait list for a large party was long. Kelsey squealed when another name cancelled.

Running into Cole was pure luck in motion. Kelsey doubted Cole remembered that the last time she visited Maxi's Place. Cole dropped colorful and suggestive hints and she'd fantasized about them ever since. This time, her crush was deep and she was very aware that slowing down was her only option tonight.

The party was over when Debra started to nod off. Cole sat down next to her and smirked at the intoxicated bachelorettes. Those brown eyes brushed across her body with such carnal determination, Kelsey reconsidered her decision. She had a feeling that Cole could do things to her body she's never experienced. She almost returned the inviting gaze but steeled her resolve instead.

"I hope you have a designated driver." Cole said.

Kelsey smiled. "How sweet of you to worry, but no, I did not trust my life with anyone in this group of lushes."

She nodded and licked her lips. "Well…since they have a limo, I can make sure you arrive home safely."

Her brain and pussy were in a tug of war with her sanity. "As much as I would love to accept your offer, I should make sure Debra gets home safely."

"You're a good friend."

"I try to be." Kelsey slid her business card into Cole's coat pocket. "Why don't you call me and we can get together. Just the two of us."

"Maybe I'll do that." Cole waited while she signed the credit card receipt and then helped situate passengers in the white, stretch limousine.

"I hope to hear from you." She kissed Cole lightly on the cheek.

"I would like to finish what we started."

"I would too."

"But if it weren't for your friends…" Cole grinned.

"Well, there is that, however," Kelsey returned her smile. "You should never go to the grocery store hungry."

Cole watched the limo pull off and fingered the card in her pocket. *Grocery store, huh.* It was obvious Kelsey wanted to stay out and play but when the alcohol wore off, her better judgment returned. She chuckled at the gutsy move. Any other night, Cole would've tossed the card into the trash and make the chick doubt they ever made a connection. There was always a standby at the ready. Maybe it was the thrill of the chase or that Kelsey succeeded in her quest for attention, but Cole slipped the card into her pocket with every intention of using it.

CHAPTER SIX

Logan collapsed on the couch as soon as she stumbled through the door. She had outlandish dreams about cleaning the bar. In one nightmare, Logan was wearing her strap and nothing else. Cole yelled at her for being late and demanded Logan dance on top of a box. Someone stuffed a few dollar bills in her harness. When she looked down, those eyes stared back up. Logan awoke suddenly. Disoriented, she looked around the living room. The faint glow in the room came from the neon sign across the street, filtering in between the white mini-blinds.

She rubbed the sleep from her eyes and checked her phone. No messages. No missed calls. And it was after midnight. Her body didn't know if routines even existed anymore. The cupboards were half empty since grocery shopping never seemed to be a part of the day. Logan made a peanut butter and jelly sandwich. She flipped through the channels before settling on a fitness infomercial. Logan glared down at her midsection and the tell-tale pooch that was forming. She didn't have time to work out. Logan was in a constant state of readiness. She would call at any time and Logan dutifully answered every single call or text message. She held back tears. Why was this happening again? History was repeating itself. *It doesn't have to be.* That one phrase held the jeweled prize Logan didn't know she was searching for. Who knew one sentence could be so catastrophic and life changing. Logan remembered the initial confession as she contemplated having heard correctly.

"Excuse me?" Logan said after a long silence.

She coyly shook her head. "You heard me."

"But you're married."

"What does that have to do with me and you?"

Logan processed for a moment. "So what you're saying is that you want to fuck me on the side?"

"You used to pick up things so much quicker than this." Allie teased and sipped her wine.

"I just want to make sure I heard you right."

"You act as though no one ever wanted to fuck you before."

"Maybe a casual fuck but something tells me you're thinking more long term."

"I could be." She replied. "Is that so bad?"

Logan wasn't sure. Adultery was a bad thing but the no-string thing was awesome. "Let me think about it."

Allie rolled her eyes. "What's to think about?"

"I don't break up marriages."

"Who said anything about breaking up marriages? Let me make this clear. I may not want to be married but I'm not leaving my husband." Her voice was steady. "In fact, he can never find out about this."

Logan was a little taken aback from the harsh tone and felt put in her place. Allie's demand wasn't subtle. Their tryst was sex and sex only between friends. Logan's better judgment escaped her that day. The rest of lunch was spent in a cheap motel room across the street from the restaurant. She would call or text when she could to setup a date. Often, it was the same day. One time, sex was planned by email - a very erotic email. At least twice a week, Allie stopped by Logan's apartment for a little afternoon delight. Gone were the long conversations about life, love and anything in between. Once Allie crossed over the threshold, the clothes came off and the inhibitions lowered. She left just as quickly as she came, without a soft word or embrace.

Logan was absolutely forbidden to contact her. Allie didn't want to risk meathead stumbling across random messages. Logan didn't mind, deciding at the beginning of the semester she didn't have the motivation for a traditional relationship. Their rendezvous became inconsistent causing Logan to be constantly on call. Allie had a household to take care of and a quick fuck in the middle of the day wasn't always feasible. If she wasn't at school or work, she waited at home for Allie with an open textbook in her lap. She realized the drawbacks of a sideline existence around the six month mark.

Finals were over and all those lonely night resulted in making the dean's list. Logan needed a release of stress with no options in sight. She hadn't heard from Allie in two weeks and now her brain slowed down enough to process the current situation. Great sex was an awesome benefit but where was Allie when Logan required more than a nut? She was playing Suzy Homemaker to a husband and two kids while Logan sat in an empty apartment. She wanted to let loose for winter break and waiting around for Allie wasn't an option. She craved a night out among beautiful women and a few cocktails.

She remembered the advantages of being single and decided a night out at a popular dance club was what she needed. Logan's neglected body soaked up the bass-infused atmosphere. She boogied with a healthy amount of scantily dressed lesbians in search of the same amusement. A highball of vodka and 7-Up stayed in her hand, enjoying the frank gazes from quite a few women. However, even in a drunken haze, Logan thought of Allie and how life got in the way of everything. How it should be Logan and not meathead who woke up next to her every morning. How they should be raising a family together. Suddenly suffocated, Logan pushed through the merry crowd and escaped into the unusually cool air of the early hours. The street was filled with singles, couples and the homeless guy who sat by the curb. Jim was a constant figure and knew how to play the heartstrings of the intoxicated.

"Raking it in tonight, Jim?" Logan slipped him a dollar.

"As much as I can, little lady." Jim winked, twirling the gray hairs of his beard between weathered fingers. "Catch a fish tonight?"

She shook her head. "Nope, I forgot my pole."

"Well, one thing I've learned is you can always buy another pole."

Logan stared a moment. "Yeah, I guess so. Stay warm."

She walked the short distance to the lighted parking lot and drove home, prepared to pass out. Logan refused to dwell on Jim's words of Allie's lack of communication. Tomorrow would be a new day and she would wake up refreshed. Pulling into her reserved space, she didn't see Allie until she stepped out of the car.

"Logan, where have you been?"

"Allie? What are you doing here?" More than a bit tipsy, Logan scanned her surroundings for other surprises.

"What do you think?" She hissed. "I'm here to see you but you're out whoring around."

Logan's head cleared a bit as she unlocked the door. "Whoring around? What the fuck are you talking about?"

"Do you know what time it is?"

She threw her keys on the coffee table and grabbed a beer. Allie stood with her arms across her breasts, a storm brewing on those beautiful features. Her hair was in pigtails and an overly large, trench coat hung off her body. Logan was vaguely curious as to what was underneath; however, the obvious possessive tone Allie projected touched a nerve.

"I haven't seen or heard from you in over two weeks. I wanted a little attention and got out of the house. So what." Logan took a swig.

"You know my life is limited and I can't just drop everything to come see you. I do have a family to take care of." Allie was defensive.

"Don't I know it." She snorted.

"What is that supposed to mean? You knew the deal when you agreed to it, Logan."

"Yeah, well…"

"Well what?"

"Well, I'm still single. There isn't anything exclusive between us." Logan reminded her. "You just said it. This is all about convenience and you weren't convenient to me for two weeks."

"So that's what this is about." She looked as though she'd solved some great mystery.

"What are you talking about?"

"You missed me."

The statement hung in the air for a split second before Logan snorted again. She took a long drink and avoided making eye contact. That was a side effect she hadn't counted on. The few hours she had with Allie always included a conversation about any and everything. It was though they had never parted. The distance of years and marriage melted away causing Logan to sink a little into her feelings.

"Missing you would be a bad idea, don't you think?" She finally looked at Allie and grinned. "You being married and all."

"Why can't you just admit that there is something more between us than fucking? Is that such a bad thing?"

"Because we can't have anything more than that so why pretend?" Logan answered. She partially meant what she said.

"I'm not pretending." Allie replied softly.

"Excuse me?"

"I'm not pretending, Logan."

"That isn't funny."

"I know but I didn't plan on falling in love with you."

"You're in love with me?" Her heart somersaulted against her ribcage.

Allie removed her coat, revealing a maroon pleated skirt with gold trim. Her white shirt was skin tight with buttons straining to support her ample breasts. She had on white socks up to her knees and penny loafers. It dawned on Logan the reason behind the pigtailed hairdo and an acute tightness formed in her chest. She approached Logan slowly, a wry smile playing around her lips.

"Didn't you mention something about a schoolgirl fantasy?"

"Um…" Her mouth was dry as she focused on those straining buttons. Normally available smooth words, stayed hidden in her personal lexicon.

Allie knew her breasts had Logan's attention and took her silence as consent. She unbuttoned the shirt until her chocolate mounds peeked through the virginal fabric. "I bet you could teach me a lot, Professor."

Logan's arms were around her within seconds, crushing her lips to Allie's and reaching up to twist a pigtail between her fingers. She mercilessly pushed her up against the wall, with a strange need to exert authority over Allie and wasted no time finding trimmed pussy to push two fingers inside.

"Fuck!" Allie hooked a leg around Logan's waist. She rode those fingers, matching her hard thrusts enthusiastically. "That's it."

"You don't want that." Logan taunted.

"I do want it."

"Beg me for it."

An intrigued smile played across swollen lips. "Give it to me."

"I can't hear you."

"Give it to me!" Allie began moving her hips again but Logan pulled out slightly. "Wait, don't."

"Ask me nicely." She demanded.

"Please give it to me." Aroused supplication darkened her eyes.

Logan replied with a swift push, knocking Allie's head against the wall. She didn't mind the dull ache and instead met each jab with wholehearted momentum. Her moans reverberated around the room but Logan only half heard them as she continued to unleash insecurity she hadn't known existed. Allie quickly realized the fallacy of being against the wall. Powerless, she held on the Logan's shoulders, receiving whatever was dished out and more inflamed than she had ever been.

"Oh fuck!" The first surge smacked her body and Allie reached backwards, knocking off pictures. She wildly bucked against Logan, shrieking a high-pitched staccato mixed with the occasional curse word. Finally, she couldn't hold back the levee any longer. Allie grabbed Logan around the neck and squeezed hard. The primitive glint in her eyes flaunted unexpected pleasure.

"Well, aren't we full of surprises."

Logan pushed her toward the bed. "Lay down. I'm not through with you yet."

Allie giggled and rushed to the bed. "I guess this outfit was a good idea.

Logan didn't reply and strode to the closet. She grabbed a black, plastic bag from the shelf. She purchased the leather contraption a week ago and excitedly waited for a call that never came. Now she wanted to show Allie what she'd missed. Her testosterone level increased with the click of each buckle. She adjusted the cock flush against the mound of her pussy and stepped back into the bedroom.

Allie lay on her stomach, breathing still slightly labored as she enjoyed a cat nap. Logan stared at her a moment while she unwrapped a condom. She rolled it down and squirted lube on the erect shaft. Without a word, Logan spread Allie's legs and pushed inside. Her body jerked but swiftly recovered. She rolled her hips back to greet each thrust as Logan hammered her still sensitive walls.

"Oh fuck! When...did...you...get...that?"

"Don't worry about it." Logan replied, grabbing a ponytail. She pushed deep to the hilt and enjoyed the muffled scream against the pillowcase. With one hand on her waist, Logan began a slow rhythm of pushing and pulling. Every other plunge, she dug her toes into the bed to so Allie felt every inch of her cock.

"Shit, w-whatever has gotten in to you I fuck-ing love it!" Allie reached backwards to grab at the harness only to have her hand swatted away.

"Did you ask me if you could touch it?"

Allie eventually stopped trying to keep up with the forceful jabs and surrendered to Logan's hands. She couldn't deny the multiple orgasms ravaging her sweaty body even if it was a bit rougher than normal. A shiver began at the tips of Allie's toes, traveled upward through the tense muscles of her thighs and scooted forward. Logan hooked an arm around her neck, bringing her back hard against her cock and continued to pound oversensitive flesh. She felt the ensuing eruption building within Allie but didn't stop the onslaught.

Somewhere in her subconscious, Logan knew that anger spurred her lust to new heights. However, the alcohol created a dizzying effect which fucked with her rhythm and her stomach. She fought through the mild nausea and grunted a fake spasm of pleasure before quickly pulling out. Allie scream was guttural as she collapsed to the bed. Logan stood and on the way to the kitchen, unshackled her hips from the leather contraption. She sipped the lukewarm water and cursed her dehydrated body. She will her traitorous stomach to behave and turned back to find Allie slipping into her coat.

"Shit, that was well worth the wait. I'm glad he finally went out of town." Allie kissed Logan on the cheek. "I have to run before the kids wake up."

Logan had stared at the front door for at least ten more minutes, naively wondering if Allie would come back. Another month skipped by without a peep from her and the routine quickly formed of Logan living a beck and call existence. She was completely at Allie's mercy and whenever Logan smartened up, she pulled the love card. Logan's weakness disgusted her and now she had fallen back into the trap. Her mind played games with her heart and she knew her line of thinking was slightly illogical. Logan couldn't deny she never felt this way with anyone else and for an unknown reason, she knew she never would. Maybe they were moving toward something permanent.

Maybe this time was different. Maybe this time Logan made sure happily ever after became a reality.

CHAPTER SEVEN

Daniel took a deep breath and punched the virtual numbers on his cell phone. He exhaled shakily while the annoying rings ticked down to an uncomfortable conversation. He counted the rings waiting until at least the sixth one before hanging up. Daisy picked up in the middle of the fifth ring.

"St. Clair residence."

"Daisy, this is Danny, um... Daniel."

"Danny!" Daisy squealed. "Where you been? Mama is throwing a complete fit. She called yo boss and everything."

"I heard. Where's Mama?"

"In the kitchen, cleaning chitlins. Mama! Danny's on the phone!"

Daniel heard the shuffle of own house shoes across the wooden floor. She's had those same pink flowered slippers since he was in junior high. His chest constricted as the shuffles crept closer, suddenly ashamed that he wasn't the best son anymore.

"Danny boy! Is that you?"

Her thick twang produced a brief smile. "Yes Mama, it's me. How're you?"

"Well, I'm good now that I know the prodigal son isn't lying dead in a ditch somewhere." Mama laid the guilt on thick.

"I know Mama. I'm sorry I haven't returned your calls."

"Return my calls? Danny, I didn't have the right number to even call you." She admonished. "Now are you going to tell me what's going on with you? I'm tired of guessing."

Daniel hesitated. "Nothing is going on, Mama. I'm just busy with work."

"You weren't even at work when I called." Mama sighed. "It's okay, Danny. One day you'll tell me what you're running from."

Remorse gripped Daniel's heart and the words dangled on his tongue but he didn't have the courage. "I'm sorry, Mama."

"Me too, son."

~~~~~

A dip in temperature made Bailey crave homecooking. She knew Ava wouldn't feel like cooking an elaborate meal after classes all day. Bailey didn't usually show off her kitchen skills but Ava was worth it. A nice pot roast didn't sound too daunting until she realized she hadn't made one before. So she called the one sister who knew.

"Sheila, I need your help."

Sheila hesitated. "This is unexpected."

"What is unexpected?"

"You asking for help."

Bailey laughed. "Yeah, I guess so. But for real, I want to cook a pot roast."

"A pot roast?" She asked. "For who?"

"Why does it have to be for someone?"

"Why would you cook a roast just for you?" Sheila never missed an opportunity for nosiness.

"I like roast." Bailey dodged the question.

"I don't think you like it enough to eat a whole one with all the trimmings."

"You never know."

"Okay Bailey, I'll play along. Do you have a roasting pan?"

"What's a roasting pan?"

Sheila laughed. "I'll be right over."

She showed up with not only a roasting pan but also spices, a meat thermometer and a rolodex of recipes. She dragged Bailey to the grocery store and proceeded to teach a lesson in choosing a suitable pork roast, appropriate vegetable and a nice bottle of wine. Sheila worked wonders in Bailey's kitchen that went way beyond the boxed skillet meal.

"So who is she?"

Bailey's head popped up at the question. "Sheila…"

"Look, I know you too well to even entertain the thought of you eating all this by yourself." She continued to cut onions and potatoes. "Plus you're never single and it's been a minute since I've seen you with a woman."

"So…" Bailey swiped a carrot. "All speculation."

"She must be special." She noticed the euphoric expression spread into Bailey's eyes and knew she was right. Her baby sister was in love. "Are you going to spill it or not?"

"Okay, okay. It's Ava."

"Cute little Ava from Maxi's?" She was shocked Ava gave Bailey a chance. "For how long?"

"About six months."

"Wow, where have I been?"

"Chasing boys." Bailey teased.

"Shut it." She asked the important question. "If you're just dating, why all the secrecy? Are you dating someone else?"

Bailey shrugged her shoulders. "Well for one, Cole warned me to stay away from Ava."

"You were kind of running through the hostesses for a while there."

"I know but Ava's different. She keeps my attention."

"And two?"

"This was her idea."

"Seriously?" Sheila positioned the vegetables around the roast and placed the lid on top.

"Seriously."

"That's a switch."

"I know, right?" Bailey looked through the small, rectangle oven window.

"Don't you fuck this up."

"What do you mean?"

"You know what I mean. Monogamy isn't your strong suit."

Bailey grinned. "I don't want to cheat on Ava. At least, I don't plan on it."

Sheila shook her head. "Then don't plan on it."

She departed with strict instructions on the roast completion and Bailey hovered around the oven. The sides were easy enough since most of the vegetable lay in the roasting pan. She saved the rolls for last and set a timer on her phone. Ava was due to show up any moment and she wanted everything finished and waiting. When the timer sounded, Bailey popped the rolls into the oven and basted the roast. Her stomach growled from the mouthwatering aroma and she couldn't wait to see the surprise on Ava's face. A home cooked meal is a definite increase pussy points.

There was something ominous about the way her phone rang. Bailey stared at it a moment, confused about the gripping dread. "Hello?"

"Hey baby." Ava cooed.

"Hey, almost done."

"Um, no."

"No?"

"One of the students in my group project isn't even halfway done and it's due tomorrow. The rest of the group has busted ass but we still have a few hours before it's complete."

"A few hours?"

"Baby, I'm so sorry." Ava rushed to calm her. "You know I'd rather be there with you but this grade is important to my degree."

Bailey's sigh was deep and ragged. "I understand."

"Are you mad at me?"

"I'm disappointed. I wanted to spend some time with you."

"I'm just as disappointed as you are, trust me. I'm actually pissed about it. This is the reason I hate group assignments. Besides me, Tre was the only one who completed their part entirely."

Tre was the last person she cared to hear about so Bailey ended the call soon after. The stench of burning rolls penetrated her misfortune. She rushed to the oven, grimacing at the charcoal rocks not fit for consumption. The rocks made a quick exit in to the trash. Anger and resentment floated behind her eyes. There were too many names to count of the women who would love to spend time with her. School couldn't be this critical. Why can't that slow muthafucka get their work done? Why did Ava always have to clean up the messes? *Tre was the only one*...Bailey didn't give a flying fuck about Tre but wondered how much Ava did. Ava loved intelligence and maybe music wasn't smart enough for her tastes.

Bailey turned off the stove and pulled the roast out of the oven. A spray of steam shot out from underneath the lid and the sight of the bubbling meal incensed her even more. No longer hungry, she dumped the whole pan into the trash. Hot gravy splashed on the white wall and a brown trail dripped down onto the floor.

"Fuck this shit." She grabbed her keys and wallet, stomping out of the door in search of a little attention.

CONNECT WITH LITERARY STUD

Blog - WordPress
The Musings of a Dedicated Wryter
Subscribe for special offers and inside information

Website
LiteraryStud.com

Social Networks
Facebook: Literary Stud – Lesbian Author
Instagram: literarystud
Google+: Literary Stud
Twitter: @literarystud
YouTube: Literary Stud

Coming Soon!

Maxi's Place: The Web Series

ABOUT THE AUTHOR

Born and raised in Dallas, Texas, Literary Stud has honed her craft since she could form sentences. At the age of eight, she presented her mother with a short story about the funny people living in her head. Instead of committing her to a mental institution, her mother encouraged her writing and remains an avid supporter to this day. Writing became her reason for breathing but the work she produced only satisfied mainstream society. Eleven years later, Literary Stud realized her sexuality and she was no longer comfortable writing the accepted romance and the characters began to mimic the world around her.

Literary Stud has written several short stories showcasing Lesbians of color. Most feature various circumstances in Lesbian relationships with believable characters that remind you of close friends. Literary Stud brings grown and sexy to life in the serial story Maxi's Place by weaving realistic tales of Lesbian culture.

Maxi's Place Series
Ebooks available on Smashwords.com
Rumors Ring True
It's Complicated
The Lies We Tell

Made in the USA
Charleston, SC
27 April 2014